Devil's Oak

Waking the Feminine Wound

A Short Story Collection

Advance Praise for Mary Carroll Leoson

Devil's Oak: Waking the Feminine Wound

"*Devil's Oak: Waking the Feminine Wound* is a collection of atmospheric and emotionally charged short stories that explore themes of grief, rage, legacy, and womanhood, particularly within the context of Southern culture and familial inheritance. Through haunting, lyrical prose, each story investigates what is passed down through blood, silence, ritual, and sometimes revenge. Whether it's a mother braiding secrets into her daughter's hair or a girl uncovering the violence buried beneath family traditions, the collection lifts the veil on intergenerational trauma and the resilience it breeds."

—Diane Sismour, author of novels and screenplays

"When I put the book down, I found myself thinking about the characters and wondering what was going to happen next, counting the minutes until I could dive back in again."

—Ada Wofford, Sundress Publications

"I loved Marguerite in "Devil's Oak," her personality shone through, and I found myself rooting for her immediately. I loved seeing her rebel against expectations of femininity. Go, Marguerite!"

—Janet Alcorn, author of award-winning short stories

Also by Mary Carroll Leoson

The Butterfly Circle

Exhuming the Bones Podcast

Devil's Oak

Waking the Feminine Wound

by Mary Carroll Leoson

Middle Tennessee State University

Devil's Oak: Waking the Feminine Wound

Published by *MT Open Press* (Blue Crescent Books imprint) at Middle Tennessee State University · Murfreesboro · First edition-October 2025.

Each story has been editor and press reviewed. The entire book has also been externally reviewed by experts in the field as part of the quality review process. The publisher and author disclaim all responsibility for errors. All URL links worked at the time of publication.

Identifiers
ISBN (paperback) 979-8-9995864-0-7
ISBN (hardcover) 979-8-9871721-9-3
ISBN (digital PDF) 979-8-9871721-6-2
ISBN (digital epub) 979-8-9871721-7-9
DOI: https://doi.org/10.56638/mtopb00425
Library of Congress Control Number: 2025944260
Keywords: ghosts, fairy tales, fiction, women, historical, paranormal, magical realism, creative writing, myth, legend, short story, literary horror

Cover image alternative description: A book cover with a dead tree, crow, ice covered apple, a werewolf, and bees circling the darkness. The words *Devil's Oak* are in bold red against a dark black background.

Press Operations
MT Open Press and Blue Crescent Books are imprints of *Digital Scholarship Initiatives* at the James E. Walker Library, Middle Tennessee State University. https://openpress.mtsu.edu

Director, Production Editor and cover design: A.Miller. Associate Editor: Ginelle Baskin. Cover image adaptations from Canva. Typeset in Garamond.

Digital version (PDF) available at https://openpress.mtsu.edu
Print-on-demand version (epub, paperback, hardcover) available at https://www.lulu.com/spotlight/mtop
Goodreads: https://www.goodreads.com/mtopenpress

Suggested Citation
Leoson, Mary Carroll. *Devil's Oak: Waking the Feminine Wound*. MT Open Press, Middle Tennessee State University, 2025. https://doi.org/10.56638/mtopb00425

A Note

This collection features horror fiction. As such, this book may contain scenes, themes, and representations that some readers might find disturbing.

The stories and characters in this work are fictitious. Certain long-standing institutions, agencies, and public knowledge are mentioned, but the characters involved are intended for fictional storytelling purposes.

Table Of Contents

Dedication

To Becky, who walked by my side as a maiden and who still does.

To Korinne, who moved me into motherhood and grandmotherhood.

To Lynn, who planted the seeds of wisdom and who now guides from the other side.

To my mother, grandmothers, and beyond – I hope I have carried forward your love and helped to heal your wounds.

And to Ed, always.

Foreword

by Christopher Barzak

It is a rare privilege to be able to witness and introduce the emergence of a voice as special and resonant as Mary Carroll Leoson's. Mary's stories are rooted deeply in the soil of ancestral memory and the landscapes of the American South, yet they reach far beyond that geography into the universal territory of trauma, resilience, and transformation. From the opening pages of this collection's introduction, where the figure of Eira—the crone, witch, and protector—emerges from the winter orchard, to the visceral and unsettling scenes beneath the gnarled branches of Devil's Oak itself, Mary's prose is both lyrical and unflinching. She invites readers to confront the shadows that linger in the margins of history and the American psyche, to listen to the hum beneath the glistening surface of our lives, and to recognize the wounds that have shaped and sometimes shattered us, individually and collectively.

What distinguishes Mary's work is her ability to inhabit the liminal spaces between myth and reality, past and present, the seen and the unseen. In stories like "Devil's Oak" and "Honey Tree," the natural world is alive with spirits, memories, and magic, serving both as sanctuary and battleground for the people who inhabit these spaces. The live oak, with its knotted bark and whispered secrets, becomes a symbol of endurance and ancestral connection, while the honeybees in "Honey Tree" carry the collective wisdom and sorrows of generations. These stories pulse with a deep empathy for women's experiences of violence, loss, and reclamation, without ever succumbing to despair.

Mary's narrative voice is one of both tenderness and ferocity. She does not shy away from the awful realities many of her characters face, whether it is the violence inflicted upon Marguerite or the spectral presence of the Marsh Girl who embodies pain and vengeance. Within these dark places, though, there is also determined hope, a call to awaken "the feminine wound" not as a mark of brokenness, but as a source of power and renewal. This is a collection that demands to be read with both an open heart and a keen mind, as it challenges us to reconsider the stories we tell ourselves about womanhood, trauma, and survival.

I am continually impressed, too, by Mary's rich understanding of folklore, history, and the complexities of identity, but it is her fearless perspective and emotional honesty that make these stories sing like no others, honoring the voices of women who have been silenced, erased, or misunderstood. Reading these stories, I was reminded of the power of storytelling to heal and to transform our lives, even in the darkest periods we may walk through, alone or together. Mary Carroll Leoson's stories are a testament to the magic that lives and grows within the wounds we all carry. It is my honor to introduce you to her unforgettable voice through the darkly enchanting stories in this collection.

Introduction

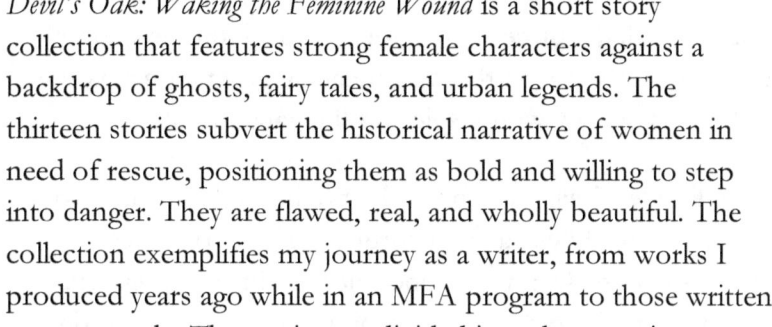

Devil's Oak: Waking the Feminine Wound is a short story collection that features strong female characters against a backdrop of ghosts, fairy tales, and urban legends. The thirteen stories subvert the historical narrative of women in need of rescue, positioning them as bold and willing to step into danger. They are flawed, real, and wholly beautiful. The collection exemplifies my journey as a writer, from works I produced years ago while in an MFA program to those written more recently. The stories are divided into three sections: Maiden, Mother, and Crone. Each section symbolizes a phase of a woman's life, exploring common overarching themes that reflect our collective unconsciousness. Some of these women mirror parts of me, but most have emerged from the ethers of the universe, begging to be born onto the page.

When some learn that I am a horror writer, they are surprised because of my sunny disposition. But it is particularly within the horror writing community that I found the support and acceptance I needed to thrive as an author. I agree with Carl Jung that creativity can give voice to the shadows within us, and as they are expressed, we become more authentic. We can release them and heal the wounds from which they emerged. Such is the power of storytelling and allowing unhealed energy to move through us and into the world, where others might relate to our secrets. Storytelling as a catalyst for community-building is also central to the courses I teach, from psychology to creative writing and literature.

Maiden

The maiden era of a woman's life often involves innocence, precociousness, and idealism. Both in stories and in real life, young women are sexualized, pressured, bullied, and manipulated; the pieces in this section touch on these ideas and explore themes of revenge, breaking generational patterns, and defying reality with magic and the paranormal.

"The Braided Veil," which was first published by Underwood Press, features Lucie, a young orphan in Victorian New Orleans who seeks revenge upon her mother's abuser. This story is one of two that I was inspired to write while visiting New Orleans with my husband. I fell in love with the doors that hid secret gardens and felt the deep history of the French Quarter. When I learned about Storyville, I was tempted to explore the dark in the old red-light district.

The second tale that came to me in Louisiana was "Devil's Oak," after which this collection is named. This story addresses the horrors of slavery through the eyes of a young girl, Marguerite, who learns that her family owned human beings. To paint an accurate picture of this horrific history, my husband and I visited the Whitney Plantation Museum, where the lives of enslaved people are honored and remembered. Some references to slave experiences in this piece, such as the German Coast Uprising, are based on facts documented at the museum. This piece originally appeared in *The Lost Librarian's Grave,* and I was honored to receive a Pushcart nomination for the story.

"Good Little Girls," which was originally published under the title "The Favor" in *Coffin Bell Journal,* takes readers back to childhood in which a sick girl explores her neighbor's attic on a stormy day; she discovers more than she bargained for. This piece was a challenge to write because of the girl's young age, but as soon as I was able to find her voice, the words flowed easily. "The Game" explores relational aggression in the 1990s in a "mean girls" style that takes a grisly turn at an abandoned amusement park. Writing this story had me revisiting high school memories of peer pressure and the "high" of taking risks. Finally, "Selkie Skin" leans into Celtic lore, following a young pregnant girl, Elizabeth, who longs for freedom from her circumstances.

Mother

Mothering can mean many things, from bearing children to nurturing stepchildren, students, friends, other family members, pets, and gardens. When one is a mother or performing the act of mothering, she often puts others before herself, sacrificing for their well-being. This can be beautiful and helpful, but it can also lead a woman to give away too much. In this way, she can be manipulated, taken for granted, or even abused. These stories explore a woman's experience between maidenhood and middle age. They focus on themes of liberation, revenge, and the mental pressure that comes with motherhood and relationships.

"The Ripper Society" reaches back through time to Jack the Ripper's wife, Florie, who discovers his misdeeds and takes matters into her own hands. This story also explores the possibility that the perpetrator may have been more than one person—a club with a dark agenda. While this is a work of fiction, there are some truths in this tale. According to Graham and Emmas, Florence Maybrick was accused of poisoning her husband, James Maybrick, with arsenic delivered via Valentine's Meatjuice (and supposedly extracted from flypaper). James Maybrick, who consumed arsenic regularly for virility, has also been accused of being Jack the Ripper. While the diary that surfaced claiming Maybrick was the notorious serial murderer has been recognized as fraudulent, mystery still surrounds this man and others who may have acted as Jack the Ripper. There are also many theories about various suspects that are equally compelling, but this particular thread begged to be untangled. This piece originally appeared in *Historic Tales: Collection of Short Stories*.

"She Has Seen the Wolf" is a novella that connects to my novel, *The Butterfly Circle*; when a graduate student learns she is pregnant, she uncovers her family's connected history to a haunted home for unwed mothers. This new story is a different timeline (1990s) than appears in *The Butterfly Circle*, so when Katie and her childhood friend, Bea, explore the home, it is in ruins but far from empty.

"Roots in the Cove" tells the story of Veronica, a woman in an unhealthy relationship who shapeshifts into a bear on a trip to Gatlinburg and finally finds her freedom. This story highlights the rage that builds in a woman who feels trapped by a romantic partner. Both "Marsh Girl" and "Cicadas in the Suburbs" explore the psychological challenges of suburban life, including postpartum depression and the longing for the magic of youth. These last three stories in this section were inspired by dear friends and their various journeys in relation to others and themselves.

Crone

As Sharon Blackie writes in her book *Hagitude: Reimagining the Second Half of Life*, a crone is "a perfect reflection of what all old women come to be in the end: the place where life and death meet" (252). Crowned with gray hair and deep wrinkles on her face, the crone is wisdom embodied. Her organic structure evidences a life well lived, perhaps with stretch marks on her stomach and an ability to hear the secret speech of nature. She sings with birds and whispers to trees, and sometimes, they talk back. She knows that to hear these messages, one must be still. Patient. Observant. These final stories celebrate the crone in all her glory.

"Honey Tree," published first by *Ethnosphere Magazine*, follows a divorcing, middle-aged woman who seeks comfort from the bees; Liadan must cross the threshold out of marriage and into the rest of her life. This story was inspired by a crabapple tree in my backyard that hums with pollinator activity in the spring. "Crow Woman" is told by a grieving widow, Brea, who is visited by a magical being. I wrote this new story to honor the Cherokee who once lived upon the land where I now reside in Tennessee. Both women experience a life review of sorts, revisiting the fragmented parts of themselves. These two stories focus on painful transitions many women experience, both resulting in loss and redefining the self.

"Ghost Apples," which originally appeared in Pumpernickel House's *The Black Door* under the title "Maiden, Mother, Crone," is the poetic finale of this collection. This story is a retelling of Snow White from the perspective of the queen; she shapeshifts into a wolf to protect a young girl who has been attacked. Eira is the ultimate nurturer and wise woman, protecting the innocent with fury.

*

Dear Reader:

This collection has been developed with two primary audiences in mind—genre readers and students of creative writing and literature.

Genre Readers

Readers who are drawn to the horror genre and subgenres such as ghosts and hauntings often tell me that they find these types of tales to be the most entertaining and fascinating. As a member of the Horror Writers Association, I completely agree, but it is worth mentioning that sometimes when a work is labeled as "horror," it is not taken seriously. This is unfortunate and can lead to readers missing out on wonderful tales written with great skill. In fact, many respected writers have found a home in the horror genre, such as Poe, Hawthorne, and even Louisa May Alcott, who is best known for *Little Women*; most people are not aware that Alcott wrote a great deal of what she referred to as "blood and thunder" tales.

Horror stories can be both genre and literary in nature, and they often address wounds that need to be healed within individuals, communities, and greater society. Author Catriona Ward sums this up well, offering that "horror deals with big, subterranean feelings, the feelings we shy away from as adults – fear, grief, trauma" (para. 3). Dark fiction is a safe space to explore such emotions. My approach to writing horror is a braiding of magical realism, hauntings, and darker versions of well-known fairy tales. These tendrils of story reach past the boundary of the expected, leading readers into Freud's notion of the uncanny and Kristeva's abject horror. Ghost stories specifically can break the rules of reality and move a story beyond the here and now into the unknown, where individual and collective healing can happen at both the conscious and unconscious levels of psyche. I invite you to walk with me in this liminal space.

Creative Writing & Literature Students

As a Lecturer in the English Department at Middle Tennessee State University (MTSU), I am privileged to teach courses in creative writing and themed literature classes, such as "ghosts and folklore" and "gothic and horror." The *Devil's Oak* collection is one optional text for both ENGL 2500 Introduction to Creative Writing and ENGL 2020 Themes in Literature and Culture. In creative writing courses, students examine focal texts (specifically short story collections) that demonstrate skillful use of literary elements; these exemplars serve as inspiration for students to find their own voices as writers. Other options for the creative writing courses include texts such as *Friday Black* by Nana Kwame Adjei-Brenyah, *The Things We Lost in the Fire* by Mariana Enriquez, and *Never Whistle at Night: An Indigenous Dark Fiction Anthology*. In the themed literature courses, the focus is more on literary analysis and developing insights and arguments about the value of literature to society and culture. Other popular texts chosen for this course include Stephen Graham Jones' *The Only Good Indians*, Tananarive Due's *Reformatory*, Jesmyn Ward's *Let Us Descend*, Silvia Moreno-Garcia's *Mexican Gothic*, and Shirley Jackson's *The Haunting of Hill House*.

I have been humbled by the thoughtful analyses students have developed in response to my novel, *The Butterfly Circle*, another optional focal text for ENGL 2020. I hope that the *Devil's Oak* collection gives them more material to explore. I encourage students who choose my work to set aside the fact that I am the author, because, as we discuss in this course, there is a whole theoretical approach that encourages a symbolic "death of the author," which is much less gruesome than it sounds (i.e., Barthes and New Criticism). Rather than literal death, this lens focuses the reader's eye on the text itself, without backstory, author explanation, or rationale.

Students choose their focal texts as well as specific theoretical lenses through which they examine literature. After reading their chosen focal texts, they work alone or in groups to develop academic essays, oral presentations, and multimodal artifacts illustrating their insights and arguments. Last semester, a delightful group of students developed a card game based on the four main characters in *The Butterfly Circle*, and another inspiring group designed a collage that incorporated painted symbolism from the novel and three-dimensional paper butterflies made of pages from the book. Their discussions centered around the characters (four pregnant teenage girls), the setting (1948 in a haunted unwed mothers' home), and other literary elements. They mostly used feminist theory and psychoanalytic theory to analyze the novel. Finally, they developed insightful arguments about why the novel is relevant to today's society; some suggested that it could be used as a basis for talking about contemporary inequities while others focused on the religious aspects of the novel.

I hope that literature students who choose the *Devil's Oak* collection as a focal text find the stories to be equally as compelling and relevant to today's society, even those stories that are historical in nature. Additionally, for creative writing students who choose the text, I hope that they are inspired to develop their own characters who are deeply rooted in active setting. With each story they write, I hope they find new layers of their own unique voices.

All Readers

I believe storytelling is crucial to teaching, to connecting with others, and to healing individual and collective wounds. I have found such healing particularly through writing historical fiction that weaves fairy tales, ghost stories, and a combination of darkness and light. I offer this collection to you, dear reader, as a celebration of all women and the numerous roles they play. Being a woman in our contemporary world comes with many challenges, some which lie hidden beneath lipstick and mascara, and some that inflict deep scars. My hope is that you may find a reflection of yourself or someone you love in these pages, and through this sharing, some of the shadows are released into the world for healing. And as you age, as you experience loss, remember to sing to the birds and whisper to the trees. They might just respond.

Thank you for spending your time with my words. I hope they linger long after you close the pages.

~ Mary

Works Cited

Blackie, Sharon. *Hagitude: Reimagining the Second Half of Life*. Novato, New World Library, 2022.

Graham, Anne E. and Carol Emmas. *The Last Victim: The Extraordinary Life of Florence Maybrick, the Wife of Jack the Ripper*. London, Headline Book Publishing, 1999.

Ward, Catriona. "Catriona Ward and the Power of Writing Horror." *The Novelry*, 2 October 2022, https://www.thenovelry.com/blog/writing-horror. Accessed 9 June 2025.

Whitney Plantation Museum. Whitney Plantation, 2025, https://www.whitneyplantation.org. Accessed 10 July 2025.

Part One: Maiden

"Do not think me a maiden who needs saving from a dragon.

I am the dragon, and I will set the world aflame."

~ Sydney Marie Hughes

The Braided Veil

New Orleans, U.S.A., 1898.

Lucie wove the fine hair between her fingers and around thin wire, its softness slipping across her skin like a mother's caress. The rhythm charmed her, begged her mind to visit times gone by, invited her to stay. Her fingers moved of their own accord, as they always did when she crafted hair pieces, and now this masterwork. Her attention hummed as it dipped into the past, luring her from her body. Each memory brought the smell of soft perfumes, taste of warm milk, sound of a gentle lullaby. But as soon as her mother's face came into focus, the reverie dissipated as smoke, wafting into the ether.

And she was alone again with her task, braiding and dreaming and weeping for what once was.

She had long ago filled the tear catchers; their crystal hollows brimmed with salty liquid that might never vanish. Her mother had been gone for almost three months now, poisoned by the laudanum that had called to her so. It loved her too much. Just thinking about it now made the girl's body yearn. A sweet red apple begging for a bite, tart beneath the skin, with hints of spice. Bitter cinnamon swirled against merlot in her memory with honey and saffron notes.

Lucie batted at the sensations, banished them. She resisted the nectar's kiss—something her mother could never do.

Her mourning persisted from dawn to dusk, breathed its way into every moment, nestled in beside her under the bed sheets, then reached into nightmares. She longed not only for her mother, but her mother's confidantes, those who had taken Lucie in like aunties. She'd lost them one by one to the dragon's nectar.

Now nights blended together, cloaked under a veil of braided threads. Ebony, chestnut, fire, gold, and taupe. They shrouded her face in intricate lace, woven memories of the women who'd sprouted the hair. She called each into her mind, whispered their names, saw their lifeless forms frozen in the wake of seduction. The poison ran thick in their blood, a weight that finally dragged them below the surface and into the pool of death. Now all that remained were their tresses.

The veil was an ornate headpiece, woven of their collective locks, her mother, Clara's, the most prominent. The crown was a wreath of intricate reverse chain, striped snake, eight square, and flat twist braids winding back and forth in flowers and coils. The plaited fringe that hung below swayed before her eyes, obscuring her features. She wore it like armor, for while others thought her in hiding, it cloaked dark intentions.

It was a mask for revenge.

*

Lucie locked the gate to the courtyard garden behind her and tucked the skeleton key into her sash. The French Quarter streets were alive with passersby returning from dinner and salons. Gas flames flickered as she passed, her matte crêpe dress soaking up the light and reflecting none of it. The mourning clothes enveloped her in shadow, made her all but disappear against darkened doorways. An unaccompanied woman at this time of night was a rarity in Vieux Carré, but she feared neither seduction nor death, for she had already bested them both.

As she walked up Toulouse, turned down Rampart, and made her way toward Basin Street, Lucie imagined her life summed up in *The Times-Picayune* headlines if she was to be caught: "Daughter of Dead Storyville Seamstress Wanted for Murder." If that was her fate, then so be it as long as she took the Devil down with her.

She was only fourteen but had a fire in her belly and bitterness in her heart. She had lived and wept more than most women in their twenties. Her father passed before Lucie was even born, but her mother had always been there, had always protected her. The girl's earliest memories were of maternal hands sewing—pinning, cutting, threading, stitching. Her mother put food on the table by performing less than desirable work, fitting gowns for women of the night in the lascivious Storyville District.

Thus, from a young age, Lucie was accustomed to seeing the naked female body with its soft curves and delicate silhouette. And by seven years old, she was fashioning her own costumes, of materials both traditional and unexpected. The demand for other artistic endeavors grew, as male appetites for women with more elaborate hair and less clothing increased. The child was innocent of the vice she served and saw only adorning the body and its pinnacle with beautiful ornaments. But time and proximity had opened her eyes.

Eventually she saw things not meant for the innocent—bodies contorted in pleasure, pain, and in-between. She'd witnessed violence that went unpunished, and how easily powder and blush covered bruises and cuts. She'd watched as the women she called Auntie were seduced by vicious substances that gripped their necks like boa constrictors. Then her mother was taken by the snake in the Devil's hand.

Now Lucie plotted for his head.

As she neared the Storyville District, Anderson's came into view, its windows beacons on Rue Bassin. She passed by men on their way into the Annex, but they paid her no mind, ignoring the woman-in-mourning as if she was but a shadow.

It's exactly what she intended.

She imagined Auntie Josie inside the saloon, the loyal but calculating woman leaning against the bar delicately as she surveyed her "nieces," the working girls endearing themselves to men. "Sazerac," she'd purr to the bartender, who would have a glass already in hand for the madame. Lucie longed to visit her mother's friend but dared not reveal her presence.

The girl was careful with her footing as she crossed the cobblestone street and followed the cast iron gallery to the back of the bordello. Joyful jazz notes floated into the night with each opening and closing of the door and a lump grew in her throat as she thought of the players, with their rich laughter and dark, warm eyes. She might never offer them a fond farewell, but if she perished tonight, it would be an exit no one would forget.

She shook such notions from her mind, chided herself for losing focus. In punishment, teeth gnashed down hard on her tongue, the thick taste of blood fueling her lust for more.

She would not leave this place without taking him down with her.

A hush fell as Lucie left the bustle behind her, rounded the corner into the back alley where rats scurried and tainted fluid dripped. Her heart quickened and she gulped down fear that tested her will, begged her to retreat. From within her sash she pulled her father's pocket watch, the only thing she had from him; it said she was right on time.

She caressed the glass vial that hung between her breasts, just above her heart, where it soaked up more wickedness while it lay in wait. Lucie's pink lips curled at the edges as she considered the liquid death inside—the sticky purple juice she'd extracted from the belladonna berries. She'd cultivated the "beautiful lady" from seeds, nurtured it like a proud mother until its purple bells wept with dew and its dark berries bulged on pentacle beds.

How poetic that a beautiful lady would take his life.

When she saw him exit his apartment behind the Annex, then disappear around the corner for a night of sin and debauchery, she snuck inside to await his return.

*

The Devil's lair was a clammy room that stank of bachelor, tobacco smoke, crawfish and spices. While the latter two might normally appeal to Lucie, the combination with the prior was putrid. But as the night wore on and she sat in the dark, her senses dulled to the stink and for that she was glad.

She toyed with the idea of lighting the gas lamp but aimed to leave no trace of her presence. So, she did her work by the light of the full moon, streaming in through the window. It cast a heavenly glow on the table—an angel come to bless her task.

She uncorked the bottle from which she'd seen him imbibe on prior occasions. It once held Peychaud bitters, an amber glass container with an aged label. Now it was his chalice for laudanum, that bittersweet nectar that had stolen her mother. She emptied the contents out the window then replaced them with a combination of wine and belladonna for his evening dose.

Now all she had to do was wait behind the closet door and hope he drank before noticing a difference in flavor.

*

When the Devil stumbled into the apartment hours later, Lucie was kneeling on the closet floor, the veil beside her. She welcomed the pain in her legs for it meant she was still alive— she just had to endure the discomfort a moment longer. She watched him light the oil lamp through the cracked door, casting long shadows onto the wall, then held her breath as he reached for the bitters jar.

His mouth opened and he sipped.

Down the liquid went.

With each moment that passed her blood pumped harder and her smile grew until her teeth were bared in a jubilant growl. Her fingers enclosed upon the braided veil and pulled it to her crown, planted it there like a laurel wreath. Then she pushed the door open slowly, the creaking hinge crying as it swung.

He turned in alarm, his golden curls catching the lamplight, shimmering with an unearthly hue. His strong jaw and hazel eyes had captured many in his web, as only a Devil could. He wobbled on his feet, unsteady from the night's absinthe but not yet feeling the poison. His eyes were almond slices, narrowed and searching for movement. His handsome face was a trick of the mind for his soul was sick with rot.

"Who's there?" he said, reaching for a chair to steady himself.

She giggled like a child, a tinkle of a sound in the manly chamber, unwelcome and unfitting. Perhaps that's why it scared him so.

He jumped back, stumbled, then righted himself again.

The words crept from her mouth in a lullaby, soft and alluring despite their message. "I've brought you a present to eat you from the inside out," she said.

"I said who's there!" His voice was commanding now, a lie masking his fear.

Lucie moved into the room, aware her silhouette looked not like a woman. It devoured the light from the lamp, her charcoal dress larger than the petite form it cloaked. The braids swung in front of her face, calling to her prey, ensnaring him, enticing him into mesmeric sleep.

"Witch," he choked before leaping to his feet and bounding toward the door.

But she got there first, throwing herself against the exit, not caring that it hurt, desperate to keep him trapped. They struggled but her small frame was no match for his panicked bulk.

When her head hit the wall, she heard a crack then everything went dark.

*

Lucie heard his heaving before she opened her eyes. It was followed by a groan and the smell of vomit was rank in the air. When her lids lifted her gaze fell on the dark night sky outside the window; the moon had hid her face. Her head pounded with vigor and the taste of blood was upon her lips. She glanced down to find only her chemise and an overabundance of naked cream skin.

The Devil had torn her clothes and maybe more. It was a heavy price, but the belladonna had begun her attack. He writhed on the floor like the snake he was, victim to the exorcism.

"What did you do, wagtail?" he growled. When he looked at her his eyes were almost black, pupils consuming color.

"Peeling you from the inside and hoping you feel one painful rip for every life you've broken."

The insults continued to fly from his mouth between sins that escaped in a web of mucous and blood. Lucie watched as she gnawed at the meager knot at her wrists, ripping and pulling until she was free. The binding left bruises behind, tender and purpling, but her work was not yet done.

She approached him slowly, a wounded animal retching and writhing, then begging for mercy. "Make it stop!" he cried, his black eyes pools of emptiness, his golden locks dripping with sweat.

With each step she whispered their names in a chant, mumbling at first, then growing louder as she closed the distance between them.

"Clara. Gertie. Sabine. Rita. Camille."

"What?" He croaked the question.

She bared her teeth. "Clara. Gertie. Sabine. Rita. Camille."

His face contorted into understanding. "The whores?"

Forcefully, she repeated: "Clara. Gertie. Sabine. Rita. Camille."

"Every man on this street gives them laudanum. Not just me!" he shook his head, tried to scramble away.

She shrieked: "Clara! Gertie! Sabine! Rita! Camille!"

Her spit was upon his face and the braided veil was in her hands. She stretched the crown out like a band, plaited fringe waving in celebration, catching the flame from the oil lamp, shining ebony, chestnut, fire, gold, and taupe.

She whispered slowly, the names drawing together as one. "Claragertiesabineritacamille…" The mantra became a growl the tighter she pulled the ligature.

As his black eyes rolled up into his head for the last time, the braided veil relaxed across his neck like a banner, a masterwork fulfilled.

Lucie stared down at the man, broken and limp, no longer a Devil. His eyes would remain open—staring into death forever. With a kitchen blade, she sliced a link of curl from his brow and she conceptualized a new design. His would be the first of many hues to be captured in her next woven prop—one with an evil destiny.

Then she donned her dark clothing once again, cloaked in shadow, trophy tucked in her sash. She replaced the braided veil to hide her wicked smile and she walked back home to her garden, for she and the beautiful lady had more work to do.

This piece originally appeared in *Black Works Underwood Press*, Fall 2020.

Devil's Oak

Louisiana, U.S.A., 1903.

Marguerite dreamed of the tree long before she touched it.

Its bark was rough beneath her hands, mountains and valleys of jagged teeth under blankets of soft Spanish moss. It stretched over grass like a cloud, its shadow looming, its branches octopus arms hanging low to the ground. Its leaves sang to her in the breeze, its gentle tune in harmony with the insects nestled there. She'd wake from climbing its branches, leaves tickling her face.

It was a tree for stories, for late lunches on hot summer days, for secrets and first kisses. It held all these memories for her family—at least that's what her Mama said. She'd see for herself one day, maybe take her own beau there. Walk in the footsteps of their long-gone matriarch, Grandmére Marie, lady of the plantation.

As Marguerite grew, the sigil burned in her mind. It was hope amidst the humdrum of chores and lessons. She was southern royalty, her Mama said, born to one of the most elite families in Louisiana. They had but to return to the land for her to remember—and for it to remember her. They no longer held the plantation in title, but the earth would recognize their blood, bless them with its bounty.

*

It was during her fifteenth year that Marguerite returned to the family home. She and her Mama were distinguished guests of the new owners, the Habers, who ran the plantation with sharecroppers. They traveled from Alabama to Mississippi to Louisiana, all by train. Once they arrived in New Orleans, it was another several hours in an automobile out to the land, just paces from the Mississippi banks. Marguerite imagined what such a trip must have been like before, on horseback or wagon alone. She grimaced, thanked the Lord for her family's connections. Those were rough times for rough souls.

Her Mama had painted pictures for her mind—a sprawling land with sugar cane and billowing trees under a blue sky—a place of promise. Lavish dinners around a fancy table, music and servants, a grand four-poster bed fit for a princess. An alliance was all it would take to regain their station—a marriage to one of the Haber sons.

She wore her Sunday best on this trip, a blue gown of the finest silk with a red ribbon encircling her small waist. "Like a bow on a gift," her Mama said. The dress was more expensive than even the china upon which they ate.

It was a lie.

They had nothing—not since Father was taken by tuberculosis. He was only a hazy memory now, weak around the edges and shifting in her mind's eye. Now, Mama was almost out of favors from kind folk.

"Best to present as the royalty you are so they can see your potential," Mama said. "Bending the truth delicately is all women have ever done."

Marguerite left Alabama expecting the promised land—a husband, a reclamation of their rightful property—victory. But what she found at the gate of the old plantation felt like doom.

*

Tall leaves waived at her over the arms of white fencing, their pointy ends like fingers begging her closer. They leaned with the wind, whipped around to face her, snapped to attention under her gaze. They stretched to the sky, gray and threatening, begging for death.

She could not tear her eyes away from the sugar cane reeds. They were ugly, wild. *This* was what had brought her family fortune? The fields choked close to the mansion, ready to swallow it whole, with only fencing shackling it at bay. But as they approached her old family home and the cane fell into the background, Marguerite's eyes grew wide. This was more like the fairy tale her Mama had spun.

They drove beneath a canopy of trees toward the two-story mansion. A grand porch stretched the entire length of the second floor, supported by stately white columns. Two large cisterns stood on either side of the house as guardians, catching rainwater from the roof, holding it there to wash sins from bathers. Upon closer examination, the manor's face was marble and decorated with intricate paintings, many of which, Marguerite would later learn, were branded with her great-great-great grandfather's initials. He'd put his mark in many places, and where he missed, his wife added it, even after his death.

As they pulled up in front of the house, remnants of a passing shower gathered in puddles, waiting to spoil her pale blue gown. She fidgeted in her seat, eager to stretch her legs but unwilling to mar her clothing. She twisted the red ribbon that circled her waist, ready to leave a long trail behind her as she walked. Her mother turned to examine her, looked disapprovingly at her daughter's handiwork.

"Let it be, child. Don't fray the satin," she said.

The young man who carried a rolled rug toward the automobile was handsome. His pale eyes met hers, crinkled at the corners with his smile. His yellow hair was combed nicely, his face clean-shaven, his hands steady as he covered mud with the decoration.

"I am Stephan, my lady," he said, holding out a soft, unscathed hand to her.

She accepted it and her Mama nodded her approval.

*

It was after formalities had been exchanged and Marguerite had her things delivered to her room that she snuck away to explore the grounds. As she moved further from the big house and onto the land, she breathed in wild things waiting for discovery.

The mangled live oak was a terrible beauty. It rose from the horizon higher and higher as Marguerite drew close. It stood on the far end of the property, past the fields, work areas, and old slave quarters—now homes to sharecroppers and their families.

Finally at its foot, her breath caught in her throat. It was even more mythical looking than she had imagined, for a girl's mind can only create so much. There was a feeling she did not expect—a hum that rose within her chest in time with beating hearts that lay on the other side of the veil. Her ancestors, watching over her, whispering her name, recognizing their blood. She felt them standing beside her, a ring of entwined hands around the sacred tree.

The trunk was thick and knotted, filled with crevices and dark places for sneaky things. Her eyes caressed its bulk, resting on indentations like pockmarks, where dark moss gathered. She wiped it away from one hollow to reveal a stone embedded in the bark. It was marked with initials—M.H. She located another, and yet another, each carved with different monograms, each symbolizing someone in her family.

Her gaze traveled up the trunk, into the tangle of gnarled limbs. Her Mama's words came back to her. "They say the live oak is evergreen, for when a leaf is ready to die another takes its place, carrying on its mission." Leaves, young and old, waved at her, courted her with a gentle hiss.

She sat at its base, her back against the trunk, soaking in its shade from the fashionably late sun. The roots had drunk most of the rain, but she'd placed a mat beneath her backside for comfort. And she pulled out her book, red cedar pencil, and began to draw.

*

When Marguerite woke, she was surprised to find the sun almost setting. The evening creatures were lulling with soft tunes; frogs, crickets, and owls creeped in the shadows. She gathered her things and followed the path back toward the house, its windows like beacons in the distance.

She passed the outbuilding behind the manor, the external kitchen brimming with delicious smells and rich laughter. Her eager stomach growled, and she peeked in to see three dark-skinned women preparing food. She offered them a smile, but they looked down on their work, averted her gaze. Their bodies stiffened, their laughter was squelched. She was an outsider.

"Forgive my intrusion," she muttered, and continued on her way.

*

Dinner inside the big house was formal, though Marguerite was in no mood to enjoy it. The chiding she'd received from Mama had dampened her spirit. "You are not to run off with the forest beasts, young lady. What will they think of a girl returning to the house after dark? Shame on you."

"I merely wanted to visit the tree—"

"Not one more word, Marguerite Isabelle. Mind your Mama."

And that was that.

Marguerite behaved as was expected of her, using the correct piece of silver for each course, daintily sipping wine from crystal, dabbing at the corners of her mouth with an embroidered napkin. She laughed when appropriate, asked questions and feigned interest in all topics of conversation, and graciously thanked her host and his sons for their hospitality. She even demurely flirted with the blond son, the eldest, who she did find handsome. But her mind was drawn back to the out kitchen. To the laughter. To the warm, rich voices. To the beautiful dark faces that fell when they saw her—like she'd infected them.

"Sir, if I may," she began at a lull in conversation. "Who are the women in the outbuilding? The cooks? Are they in your employ?"

The gentleman was surprised by the question but not offended. "Why, yes, my dear. When the War of Northern Aggression ended and our way of life was interrupted, we retained some people as sharecroppers, some of their wives and daughters as help around the plantation."

Mama shot her daughter a warning glance and said in a lighthearted tone: "Such serious conversation, Marguerite. You're liable to bore us to tears." Her laughter tinkled above the table like a bell and the others joined in, though nothing was funny.

And Marguerite wondered how it would feel to eat dinner with the women from the out-kitchen instead, surrounded by their warmth. The laughter here was loud but empty.

*

The girl climbed into the elevated, four-poster bed and was almost swallowed by the feather comforter. She sank into its softness, feeling the luxury around her like a warm embrace. A gentle breeze whistled in through the windows, shifting the sheer curtains, making the flame on her bedside candle dance. It dripped wax onto the pewter candlestick holder in a long tear.

She placed her book on the pillow and turned to the pages that held drawings of the tree. The sketches were ethereal, a sample of bark, a hint of the canopy, one close-up study in leaves that looked like fingers. A single acorn, the dark bottom like chocolate with a pale caramel cap. But when she turned the page to begin a new drawing, an image peered out that she did not remember making.

The sketch captured the tree from its base, looking up into a monstrous canopy that spanned the whole sky. It loomed and crawled, leaking off the edges of the page, hungry. And as she turned the book in her hands, examining the pencil strokes on paper, the various grains that she did not consciously know how to make, the eye came into focus. It peered out from between the branches like the center of a storm, untamed and angry. The branches framed it, hugged it, crinkled around it in fury—the eye of the devil himself that looked upon the land.

An eerie cry came in with a gust through the open window.

"Oh!" she exclaimed. Marguerite jumped, slammed the book shut. She jumped again when a second gust spit hot wax from the candle, spraying it onto the table. The firelight blinked but continued to burn.

She strained her ears to catch another sound. Bugs chirped, leaves sang, but there were no human voices, nothing but the late summer night. She decided it was just her imagination. But as she fell into dreams, she was brought back to the devil's eye and what it had seen.

The fire burned brightly in the path before the slave quarters. A white man walked toward the gathering of dark-skinned children. They were afraid at first, but then they saw the sweets and their eyes grew large with delight.

He served the biscuits on platters for them, dipped in the middle, filled with molasses —a treat indeed!

"Catch them with the sweets as children," the man said. "Let them grow big and strong so they'll produce sweets for you." He offered a crooked grin, something dark behind his eyes.

Marguerite woke with a sticky mouth, the taste of molasses lingering, bitter-sweet.

*

Packages came the next day, special order from New Orleans. Marguerite knew they could not afford new clothes, but Mama smiled and said, "Don't you worry your pretty head about it, sugar."

There was a dress of pink chiffon, one of white taffeta, and one of deep purple satin edged in lace. She chose the pink one to match her cheeks, which she pinched to blush, then darkened her lips with a stain.

Her dark hair hung in ringlets beyond her shoulders, courtesy of the hour she'd spent the night prior winding them around rags. Now she looked worthy of the dresses. Mama gave her a nod of approval on her way down to breakfast.

*

Marguerite offered a pleasant smile as the servant girl placed a dish before her. Her brown hair was plaited, with skin kissed by the sun, her pale eyes far away. Freckles sprinkled her nose and a small scar marked her brow with pink. She couldn't have been more than ten.

"Genevieve, we'll take more tea now," said Haber in a firm but kind tone.

"You are so generous to welcome the mulatto girl into your home," said Mama. Marguerite had heard the word before, though her Mama usually called brown children 'those people.' A foggy memory rose to the surface of a long-lost friend; they'd once shared laughter, tears, and secrets, until her Mama found out and forbade it. In her mind's eye, the child's brown fingers intertwined with Marguerite's small, pink ones, but the image was gone just as quickly as it had come, leaving only a dull ache in her chest.

Grace, she thought, that was her name.

"Genevieve is quadroon," Haber corrected her. "I do what I can to help those in need, and to make up for... certain... indiscretions."

Her Mama blushed. "Well, what a kind gesture. Isn't that right, sweet?" She leaned toward her daughter with raised eyebrows.

Marguerite nodded as if she understood, though she didn't. Something about their exchange felt dirty.

*

When she visited the oak the second time, Marguerite approached with caution. She half expected the canopy to come to life—lift a lid and reveal an uncanny watcher. But it stood frozen, like a painting in the dank southern air, haunting and beautiful. A wet mist clung to the branches, blending into the sky, blocking out the sun.

Despite the luring scene, she kept her distance, sketching from outside the perimeter of a mushroom circle. If this was her family's legacy, she should feel a sense of comfort, familiarity, home. Certainly, the beauty was endearing, but she couldn't shake the foreboding that twisted her stomach.

There was a creeping sense of being watched and the hair rose on her arms. She scanned the horizon for evidence of company but found it barren. Just the stalks waving gently in the breeze that shifted them one way, then another, a hush rising from the rhizomatic, collective consciousness that was the sugar cane. It whispered, groaned, settled back into the landscape, but never stopped breathing.

Marguerite placed her sketches aside and stood. If this was her family's land, she should not feel so unwelcome. Entitlement swooned in her chest, filling her with boldness.

She approached the tree in small steps, as if trying not to frighten a wild animal. Blades of grass tickled her ankles, the moist air clung to her skin. She swiped at a loose curl that kept returning to her forehead despite her efforts to tame it.

The roots were thick under her feet, tangled and reaching, drawing her in. She imagined the feu follet might hide there, beneath the mushrooms or inside notches in the trunk, waiting to lure her with mischievous lights.

Under its canopy, she studied the arms of branches, reaching out to the sides and up to the sky. Her eyes traced their length, searching for spiders and monarchs and sparrows. Spanish moss hung down like fine lace, graceful and delicate. And as she moved closer to the trunk, she heard the hum.

It was a dull vibration, all one note, low and consistent. Marguerite recalled the base tones of the cello her neighbor played back in Alabama and how they moved through her body, tickling her insides. She drew closer, placing her hands on the bark and leaning in until her ear was against the rough surface. The drumming was thunderous, like a million stamping feet at once. She jumped back, both startled and exhilarated by this discovery.

It was a secret the tree shared with her; she had a feeling it was one of many. She bowed in a healthy respect for its majesty before returning to bed for the night.

*

As Marguerite reclined in the billowing pillows and cozy sheets of the princess bed, she became lost in thoughts of the humming tree. Drowsiness overtook the girl before she even knew it was upon her.

The air smelled of sweat and fear and blood. It hung heavy around the Black men as they marched along the river, rage burning in their chests. They moved together as one, the fingers of a hand; this is how they would take the captors down.

Some fell, but the devils came on horseback, wielding weapons for which they had no match. If anger could kill, they would be victorious, but fury was fed by blood. So, the white men bled them, stole their spirits. They seeped into the ground, ran in streams to the river, became the snake.

Their heads were sliced crudely from their necks, placed upon poles to remind any resistance what lay in store for rebellion. The heads lined the river in decoration, a gruesome necklace for a hungry demon.

And the tree watched.

*

It was still dark when she woke from her nightmare, sweat slick on her chest, her hair matted to her neck like wet blades of grass. Her heart beat against her chest in painful thuds, like she'd been running along with the men, frightened for her own life. This was silly, she knew—to breathe life into old stories spun to scare children. They were nothing more than fairy tales. Weren't they?

The wind howled outside, angry, unsettled—like her mind.

After lighting the candle, Marguerite held it before her as she crept into the hallway, its beacon casting strange shadows about the hall. Each step creaked under her in argument, bidding her back to bed, but her stomach growled, twisted with hunger to chase the dreams away. And there was nothing more terrible to the girl than an empty stomach because she had not known worse—ever.

Before entering the kitchen, she paused before the oil painting depicting her Grandmére Marie, the lady of the plantation. It was not the first time she'd studied it, but the angelic form that had greeted her in daylight took on long shadows under the candle's glow. Her dark hair held the same hue as Marguerite's, a warm brown with hints of gold and red. Her nose had a similar upturn at the end, too, petite and round. But that's where the similarities ended. Rather, she saw her mother's face in the oils, right down to the lime green eyes. Grandmére Marie's expression was firmer than her mother's, commanding and harsh, with a wrinkle between her brows. She wore a royal red gown with white lace beneath that suggested softness but promised nothing; this was so much like her mother, too.

Urged by her stomach, Marguerite moved on to seek refuge in the kitchen, feeling the lady's gaze upon her as she crept.

*

It was when she was sneaking back up to her chambers that Stephan caught her. She was halfway up the stairs when she saw him, leaning against the wall outside her door. She flushed immediately, glad for the poor candlelight. She wiped crumbs from her lips, held her head high and tried to look confident.

As the space between them closed she became more hesitant. His eyes that had once seemed so gentle now held a foreboding about them. Brow bones above the light circles were heavy, cast shadows downward in a sinister angle. His gaze did not wander. His expression did not soften upon her approach. His bulk blocked her passage to the door.

She hesitated.

"Ladies should stay locked up in their rooms at night." His voice was a low growl. She could smell the drink upon his breath.

He moved closer, adjusted the candle in her hand to the side. His eyes examined her and she realized the light might suggest her form beneath her nightgown. She flinched, stepped back, but he caught her wrist, held tight.

"You never know what lurks in the dark on these lands," he whispered.

He held her gaze and she swallowed. His grasp loosened, his hand moved to her face, caressed it. It drifted down her neck to her collar bone, lingered there, then began to move south.

The slap landed hard on his face. It rang out with a crack that echoed in the hall but no one stirred. Marguerite used the moment of shock to pass through the door, secure it behind her, before cradling her hand. It throbbed already and she could only imagine what it would look like in daylight. It was her drawing hand.

"Full of fire." His voice penetrated the door. "I like it."

She heard him stumble down the hall, then his door close. And the tears came. He was no gentleman. He was something else.

*

Marguerite woke early and dressed quietly, hoping no one heard. It was no small feat to don her gown and lace her shoes with a sore hand, but she managed. Then she crept down the stairs quietly and held her breath until she was outside the front door and into the garden. The stone path led beneath an archway of trees and through a series of flower beds, some in bloom, some in wait. It curved to the left and led to a fountain at the edge of the property, just inside the fencing that marked the plantation line.

The water sprinkled happily from the lips of an angel, her wings spread wide. The cool stream was a prayer being sent off to the Lord, landing in a sea of hope among other wishes. Marguerite interrupted its journey with cupped hands, sipping the water to cleanse her soul. Then she stared down into the water, looking for clarity but finding only her wavering reflection.

But the sunlight sprinkled through the branches above, and the breeze was soft against her hair, so although she felt unrest bubbling inside, she tried to inhale nature's calm.

She thought of her Mama, all the dreams she'd placed on her shoulders—reclaiming the family land through marriage. But Stephan was not a good man. He was not kind, was not gentle, though his mask told a different story. He knew the right things to say, the graces to offer a lady, but underneath was something sinister.

No. She would not marry that man.

She had never said no to her Mama before. Never. But the fear grew inside, ebbing ever closer to anger. It was taking on a life of its own. She would not be condemned to Stephan's whims.

His voice emerged from the house just then, a call out to his father about breakfast. Marguerite shuttered and leapt to her feet, then darted toward the side of the big house, crushing all flowers and crawling ivy in her path. Safe in the shadow of the large cistern, she paused to catch her breath and watched as he strutted down the path like a show horse. Then he paused abruptly, turned as if he sensed something, looked in her direction. His gaze remained and Marguerite's breath caught in her throat.

Then he smiled.

And she ran.

*

Marguerite's legs were thin and not accustomed to such activity, but they quickly put distance between her and the big house. She left him far behind but Stephan's wicked grin set her heart in a bad way. His attention reached after her in an angry cloud of venom, ready to snatch her up and hold tight.

She ran past the outbuilding where the food was prepared. She ran past the blacksmith's barn and the horse-filled stables and the woodman's ax, still stuck in a stump like it had been the day before. She ran past the old overseer's quarters and the sugar cane and the bowls set out for boiling, until she reached a gravel path and her ankle gave way under her weight. She sank to the ground in a sweaty heap, the sun beating down on her brow with no forgiveness. The pain was sharp and she winced as she touched it.

When the shadow fell upon her, she tensed, but it was not Stephan who stood there.

The woman's faded dress brushed the ground and her apron was dirtied with kitchen work. Her dark eyes held concern.

"You alright?" she said and reached out a hand to the girl.

Marguerite accepted the help and hoisted herself to her feet, placing her weight on the one that would hold it. She hobbled after the woman, who helped her sit on the stairs of a small dwelling.

"May I?" she asked, gesturing to Marguerite's ankle. She nodded in return.

The woman's hands were cool at first. They moved along the ankle bones, muscles, then stopped abruptly. She closed her eyes and mumbled something Marguerite could not quite hear, and her hands became warmer. Before long the heat was almost unbearable, but as the girl winced, she took them away.

"Can you walk now?" she asked.

Marguerite hesitated, then placed some weight on the ankle, expecting the pain to shoot up her leg. But there was nothing.

Amazed, she looked to the woman in wonder, but she was already climbing the stairs to go back inside.

"Wait," begged Marguerite. "Thank you. I don't understand-" she stopped herself, realizing her words might be rude. "Thank you for your kindness."

The woman nodded, turned back to her climb, then paused and glanced back. "The tree is bad. Don't go there."

Marguerite stared back at her, wanting to ask a hundred questions, but no words came to her lips. Their eyes were locked in an embrace. Eyes like deep pools of chicory with endless bounds of strength and warmth. A face gentle and nurturing, proud and carved from worry, hard work, and mothering.

Mothering like the girl had never known.

The tears filled Marguerite's eyes quickly as the woman disappeared into the house and closed the door behind her. She brushed them away and rerouted her journey, away from the tree that haunted her dreams.

*

Marguerite wandered far to the back of the plantation, a place she shouldn't have ventured on her own, but wanted nothing more than to disappear. She spent hours there, enjoying the serenity, with many paces between her and Stephan. Her Mama would be more than cross, but the conflict had to start somewhere.

Maybe if she was less appealing, the decision would be made easily. Stephan wouldn't want her if she wasn't a proper lady. But then she thought back to his words: "Full of fire. I like it."

Her shoulders slumped as she walked, her feet sinking into the boggy mud. The land was softer here, with cattails and a film of moss on rocks and roots alike. As she walked, she crafted a plan to make herself terrible—dirty and unkempt.

She came upon the swamp with little warning, the stench of decaying things and rotten eggs reaching her first. The land sloped downward into a mass of murky water and cypress trees. The tented trunks had deep ridges and disappeared beneath the water, while the thin treetops reached to the heavens, coated in shawls of gray Spanish moss.

A symphony of insect sounds filled the air, creaking, chirping, and buzzing. The lull was disturbed only by the sucking mud releasing her shoes as she stepped. They were ruined, muddied and ugly; it was just the way she wanted to return.

She scooped up the tainted water, including the squishy silt upon which it lay, and smeared it down her cheeks. She scooped and smeared in a ritual, bathing herself in the dank mixture until she was of the swamp. Then she turned to head toward the big house and to the reception that waited.

*

It was a long trek back and the sweat mixed with swamp remnants was quite unappealing, but the smell would be even more powerful to those who waited at the dinner table. It would be set with fine china atop white linen, flanked by stately silverware. Marguerite recalled the print from the other night —a gold edge encircling the cream background with dainty pink apple blossoms. The crystal glasses would be filled with sweet wine, the candles on the table casting a soft glow. In her mind's eye she saw them all seated and ready to feast— a proper banquet for a royal family.

As the lights in the windows of the big house came into view, she gathered her courage and marched without falter.

It was as she had imagined, looking through the window. Her Mama was seated to their host's left, leaning more closely than chaste. Marguerite's nostrils flared as she spied, wondering if her mother had designs of her own for marrying into the family. Had she forgotten there was already a Mrs. Haber back in New Orleans at their main residence?

At the clearing of her throat, her Mama jumped. She sat back quickly, composed herself, glanced at her daughter through the window. She cocked her head to one side, a quizzical look contorting her face.

"Well, sugar, do not linger outside. Come in and announce yourself properly," she said, and glanced at the gentleman beside her, let out an embarrassed laugh.

"Yes, ma'am," Marguerite replied and did as she was bid.

As the warm candlelight kissed her form, the audience took in her appearance. Her Mama's emerald eyes grew large in her bony face, the whites expanding exponentially. Her expression shifted from surprise to shock to outrage in a matter of seconds. Her mouth elongated then pursed, moved but no sound emerged. Then she gasped and her hand began beating the air in a fanning motion.

"What is the meaning of this?" Haber's voice filled the room and his fist pounded the table. The silverware rattled, the china clinked, and feet could be heard scuffling in the hall. His normally somber face was an angry red, bright against his graying, pointed mustache.

Stephan rounded the corner into the room, eager to see what the excitement was about. He paused in the doorway, his handsome face full of amusement at first, then changing to disgust. He held a hand to his nose and backed out of the room, disappearing into the dark.

As Haber fumed, and her Mama fainted, and Stephan retreated, it was Marguerite's turn to smile.

*

After a rough scrubbing from Genevieve, who only did so at the barking of her employer, Marguerite was banished to her room. For most of the bath, she basked in victory, knowing she had ruined all designs Stephan had about violating her purity. She would not be a prisoner under his gaze.

She was free, and yet...

It wasn't until she was tucked into bed, clean white skin under a cotton shift and soft blankets, that shame began to set in. Her heart softened to her Mama; perhaps she was not warm or nurturing, but always there with constant direction. Her

Mama was not perfect, but there was no question she loved her.

Marguerite studied the rain as it slid in graceful smears down the windowpane—a prelude into a storm that was to come. She could hear it in the distance, the rumbling thunder, followed by flashes of light against the horizon. It spoke to something deep within her, but she couldn't cry. A war was bubbling inside, and there was no room for tears.

As she relaxed into sleep, Marguerite was haunted by whispers from the past—both those of her blood and those that sought it.

The hole in the ground was like a grave, but not as wide nor as deep. It was as if a mouth had descended from the sky and bit the earth, leaving a gaping wound behind. No grass grew, no roots sought water, only worms wiggled there, writhing their way into and out of the wet soil, ingesting it and eliminating it again, but never cleansing it of its evil.

It called to Marguerite, lured her forth to its embrace. And she followed, unbothered by the mud caked on her feet or the stain that clung to the edge of her nightgown. She wanted to see what was inside, to crawl into it and curl like a newborn. But as she crested the edge of the hole, ready to step foot into the darkness, the shouting began.

In the space of moments, a dark cloud cloaked the sun and what had been stillness became chaos. The shouting grew louder, and though she couldn't decipher words, the tone was enough for terror. Marguerite ran toward the great oak tree, hid behind the trunk's bulk, and peeked out to see what was amiss.

The dark-skinned man was large, his shoulders three times the size of any man Marguerite had ever seen. His face was curled into something more than anger. He spat when he yelled and pushed the small form in front of him; it fell onto all fours, then struggled to walk upright again.

As they drew closer, she could see his victim was a woman, thin save for her protruding belly that looked like it might burst. The scraps she wore barely covered her, and she struggled to stay ahead of his wrath. Behind them both was a white man with a nonchalant gait, an expression of stone. He waived a hand in an order and his soldier passed sentence.

The woman was shoved face-down to the ground, her pregnant belly fitting into the hole there. His large arm reached back, struck toward her, a whip extending from his hand like a tentacle. The crack was sharp against her skin and left a mark that leaked around the edges. Her winces were strangled cries and with each strike. Marguerite tensed more, digging her hands into the tree's bark while shock stole her voice.

But on the third lash, she emerged from the tree's shadow, shaking and horrified and yelled at the man.

"Stop!"

Her childish voice rang in her ears but the man did not falter.

Again, she cried: "Stop!" Tears poured down her face. Either they did not hear her or they did not care. Marguerite shrank back to the tree, crumpled upon its roots, wanting to shut out the cruelty, the horror.

The beating continued, and when it was over, the woman was motionless on the ground. The white man uncrossed his arms, glanced at the tree, with the hint of satisfaction on his face.

Marguerite froze, not knowing if he could see her, if he had heard. When his eyes passed over her, they showed no recognition but the image was unmistakable. She saw her own face, from the clear blue eyes to the high cheek bones, to the brow that was rounded in a hairline that came to a widow's peak. This was her blood.

As they disappeared into the distance, leaving the woman motionless on the ground, the nausea rose up from Marguerite's bowels violently, choking her, creeping up her throat. The roots emerged from her mouth like spider legs, writhing in an effort to be born. She pulled at them and they pulled back like bony fingers, and then she woke to her own screams.

*

The fever struck in the early morning hours as the rain pelted the roof over Marguerite's bed. Her head swam with pressure, her vision hazed, but she did not know if it was the heat or the memory that scorched her mind. She could still see his face, haunting the grounds, watching as the woman was whipped, revealing the curse from which she'd been born.

Her mother was a liar. This was no sacred ground, no royal family, it was darkness. Pain. Corruption of the worst kind. It whipped mothers. It stole heads from men. It lured children with sweets until they stuck in it like bees, wanting to feed their queen.

She heaved onto the floor and the liquid burned her mouth, her nose, landed with a splash. She stared at the puddle, her widow's peak glaring back at her like an accusing finger. She closed her eyes tightly and gathered her thoughts, then she lit the candle beside her bed, wincing at its brightness. She crept to the dresser and dipped a washcloth into the porcelain bin there, placed it to her forehead and felt relief for just a moment.

But as she returned to her bed, she noticed dark fluff poking out from beneath the covers. In the candlelight it was an endless hole, waiting to suck her down into its depths to drown her in nightmares forever. Shaking off this silly notion, she pulled back the covers carefully and poked at the substance.

It was soft, a pillow of fluff. Bouncy, light, but not feathers. Even back in Alabama, the mattresses and pillows had been stuffed with feathers, no matter how their savings dwindled. There had always been that small luxury.

But this was something else.

She pulled at it, investigating the depth of the issue. Handful after handful she pulled it out, thinking at some point the feathers would emerge but it was just more of the same. She had heard of horsehair being used for such purposes in desperate times to stuff cushions for chairs and the like. As she sat with a clump of it in her hand, surrounded by the mounds she had extracted from her mattress, pillows, and even the blanket atop her, the realization dawned.

The dark texture was not the consistency of animal hair. It reminded her of only one thing. Human hair. Hair from the heads of the slaves she'd seen in her dreams, like hair from the woman who'd healed her ankle.

She had been sleeping in their remnants.

Marguerite froze. She dropped the hair in a pile where it joined the other mounds and she backed away like she'd sprung a trap. The full weight of the idea was too much for her to comprehend, too sickening for her to believe, yet there it was. She could not—would not—ignore what she saw with her own eyes. The nausea rose again and she let it, emptying her insides of the evil infecting her, releasing it from her body.

This place was a tomb.

*

Marguerite ran.

Her head pounded and her fever persisted, but she ran. Out the bedroom door and down the stairs, she ran. Through the dining area and out the back door to the stone path, she ran. Past the kitchen outbuilding, the blacksmith's barn and the horse stables, she ran. And she stopped when she got to the woodsman's ax, still resting in the stump.

It gleamed in the lightning that flashed above, winking at her, knowing. It was heavier than she expected, its wooden handle too large for one hand, so she grasped it with two. The blade aimed downward, she pulled it along as she stumbled, now weary from her sprint.

The sky grew angry, thunder bellowing, lightning not far behind. But Marguerite continued on her way, past the overseer's quarters and the boiling stations, all the way to the gravel path. She took one last look back at the big house, cisterns standing their guard on the horizon, windows still dark.

Maybe she should have burned it down with all the evil inside.

The sky cracked above, reminding her of the mission, and it released a torrent of rain that beat her brow. The drum of water striking land surrounded her, pushed her on, and even after it lessened, she could still hear its echo in her ears.

When the devil's oak came into view, it was breathing. The wind sucked its leaves one way, then the other. The roots were thick under her feet, tripping her as the wind howled her name.

What had welcomed her before now bade her not trespass.

Marguerite. The woman's voice was soft, lulling.

Marguerite. It was sweet, filled with sugar, tempting.

The girl turned away from the tree to the place where she had dreamt of the hole in the ground, where the whispers now emerged and a real hole opened. The rain slowed to a hush, the air heavy and waiting.

The woman's form was beautiful, shining. As the wind gusts returned, it floated toward her with a symphony of waving sugar cane stalks behind her. They spread quickly, sprouting from the ground in all directions, reaching out for fresh blood.

Marguerite. The voice soothed her, beckoned her, bewitched her. It was her Grandmére Marie, the lady of the plantation.

As she drew nearer to Marguerite, she found the green eyes like those of her mother. She wanted to be held, to put her head on this woman's lap and cry herself to sleep. To feel so safe that nothing could ever hurt her again. The taste of molasses was upon her lips, sticky, dripping with promise.

But Marguerite faltered. Her eyes went to the hole, and she remembered. The pregnant woman. The men with no heads. The children tempted with sweets. And she turned her gaze upon the tree.

The voice that had been sweet began to shriek. The shrill pitch went higher and higher until Marguerite wanted to scream, but still she walked forward. Sugar cane reeds struck like whips, catching her in the ankles, the arms, drawing blood.

The pain spurred her on.

Beneath the oak's umbrella, she drew back the ax with both hands and delivered a blow to the trunk. She pulled it back and thrust again, slicing the place where her grandfather's initials were. Again and again, she struck the tree until the hollow inside revealed itself.

The swarm hummed, freed of its purgatory. Against the dawn light, the bees rose into the air. The souls of the children cried, the women screamed, and the men shouted. They danced for a moment, merging into one being, a mix of joy and vengeance.

They did not need sugar; they already had honey and they fed the queen no more.

Lightning struck the tree, splitting it in two, throwing the girl from her feet and feeding the bees' fury.

The swarm pulsed with rage.

And though Marguerite stared, mouth agape, after the cloud of revenge flying toward the big house, she felt no regret.

 This piece originally appeared in *The Lost Librarian's Grave,* Redwood Press, 2021.

Good Little Girls

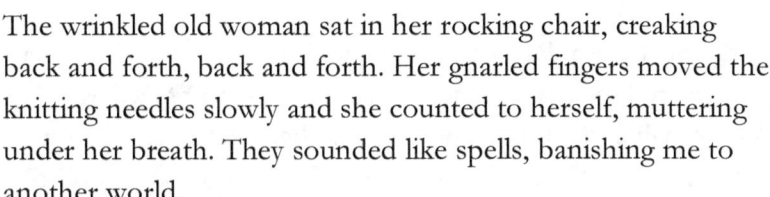

The wrinkled old woman sat in her rocking chair, creaking back and forth, back and forth. Her gnarled fingers moved the knitting needles slowly and she counted to herself, muttering under her breath. They sounded like spells, banishing me to another world.

She didn't want me there. It was just a favor for my mom, after all.

I lay on the red velvet couch under an old Afghan blanket that smelled like death. But she'd told me to do so—lie there and be a *good little girl*. When she'd felt my fevered forehead, her bony fingers were ice. When she stepped away the coolness lingered.

So, I lay there, obedient, watching her rock and knit and conjure.

Rain pelted the window outside in a steady stream, the wind howled in harmony and thunder shook the couch beneath me. The firelight played tricks on my eyes, revealing a sweet woman's face one moment, then contorting it into a skull with shadows the next. Her smile did nothing to hide the demon who peered out from shadowed sockets. A gray cat sat beside the rocker, indifferent, his green eyes otherworldly. He watched me, seemed to see things around me floating in the air. Moths? Dust? I didn't want to imagine worse.

"Back in my day, little girls wore dresses." Her croaking voice disturbed the silence. Her eyes flicked up, locked on mine, whipped back down to her crafting. "They had manners, knew when to curtsy, how to engage in polite conversation."

I held my breath. Part of me wanted to impress her, the other part wanted to stab her ancient hands with those needles. With a sigh and a roll of the eyes that had gotten me in trouble before, I tried: "Well, the weather isn't very agreeable today." The word 'agreeable' sounded foreign on my tongue, a vocabulary word resurrected from last year's writing class, but one I thought she might appreciate.

"Indeed," she said, not glancing up.

The flames in the fireplace danced and the wind howled outside. The windows rattled. The cat meowed.

"Would you like me to get another candle for you?" I offered, hoping she might see my effort at kindness. The electricity had been out for two hours now—not that there was even a TV to watch. And the old radio in the corner looked like a museum piece rather than a functioning device.

Her eyes shifted up to me, her hands not even pausing. "Young lady, my hands remember how to knit so well that I could do this in the dark. We had to make our own clothes, you know. Children today…" Her lips pursed. "You have everything handed to you."

Crabby old bat, I thought, wishing I was anywhere else—even math class with Mr. Thompson who spit on those of us in the front row when he talked. But lucky me, I had to puke on the way down the stairs this morning.

For a moment, I thought I might get to stay home alone. Mom even thought about it. I could see the wheels churning in her head. But she remembered what happened last time. So here I was, in the house time forgot.

The tall clock in the corner chimed, marking the dragging minutes.

"Almost time for tea," she muttered, more to her cat than me. He meowed at her again. "That's right, Lazarus, you'll get your treats." She stopped rocking, glanced over at me and down her nose. "I have a task for you, young lady. While I prepare a snack, you can fetch my extra needles from the attic. And another ball of yarn. My granddaughter packed them up, didn't expect me to have an apprentice. But you might as well make yourself useful—commit those fingers to something other than trouble."

I watched as she placed her project on the table beside the rocker, then braced herself to rise. As she leaned forward, her gnarled hands grasped the armrests, and she shifted her weight onto shaky legs. I shrank back, like her age was an infection.

Underneath her house dress, nylons sagged around her ankles, and I wondered if her skin also collected there. She wore sensible shoes that belonged to another time but seemed to support her well in old age.

I counted to myself as she stretched out her torso, finally standing, ten Mississippis later. Shame flushed my face as the secret part of me fantasized about toppling the chair forward, tossing her onto the floor like old laundry. I was caught between this mischievous voice and one that controlled such behavior. I imagined a devil and an angel, like I'd seen in a rerun on the Cartoon Network.

My lower lip poked out as I sulked, longing for a TV to appear out of thin air. All the delicious shows I was missing on this sick day, ever since Mom had to go back to work. Once she had doted on me, tucked me in on the couch like a taco, with one half of a comforter under me and the other on top of me. There was a little teapot reserved for sick days where she'd brew chamomile tea and serve me cinnamon toast—all that was appropriate for an upset stomach. She'd smooth my hair and place a kiss on my forehead, tuck the covers under my chin and stand guard until I fell asleep with the TV lulling in the background.

But I was ten now, too old to be babied, too young to stay home alone. Especially after what happened last time. It had taken two weeks for the charred smell to disappear.

It was a favor, she'd said. I needed to be grateful to Mrs. Miller, this stranger whose house smelled like old people. There were cold breezes that snuck in through cracks I couldn't see, strange creaking noises that crept up behind me when I wasn't looking. But Mom said I had to grow up, act like a young lady. Then she abandoned me to this ancient tomb.

"Suck that lip back in this instant, young lady." Her voice startled me. I looked up to find her looming above the couch, the skin on her face stretching down like a used candle.

"There will be no pouting in this house. You'll drink your tea and you'll like it. Now fetch me the needles and yarn from the attic."

"Fine," I muttered, trying to sit up.

"Yes, ma'am is the appropriate response," she spat, a gnarled finger accusing me.

I glared. "Yes, ma'am." If she heard the sarcasm in my voice, she didn't show it. Her small frame hobbled from side to side as she shuffled to the kitchen and disappeared through the door.

Lazarus the cat watched as I started up the steps, the wood groaning beneath my feet. The railing was cool under my hand, sticky with wax that was either cleaner left-overs or grime from other hands. My heart began to beat in my head, like it always did when I was ill. I placed my hands on my temples but they did nothing to help. I wanted to cry but knew it would make things worse. A whiner, she'd say, not as tough as children used to be.

I paused on the balcony, glancing out the peaked window to weeping gray skies. The beads of water pinged against the glass, streaked down in long trails. The cat crept up the stairs after me, watching with curious hesitation, then followed me as I continued around the bend to the second floor. The pounding in my head grew louder with each step.

As the dim light from the window diminished, the hall felt like a cave—maybe something's lair. I peered around an open door to see a canopy bed, topped in white lace. The bedspread was matching with delicate throw pillows and an aging teddy bear. There was a dressing table with delicate perfume bottles, a neat row of lipsticks, and a fancy hairbrush with a corresponding hand-held mirror. There was even a pitcher with a basin on the bedside table, like something out of a story book. It made me wonder how old Mrs. Miller really was. Ancient or not, she was stuck in the past and had nothing but disdain for children like me.

The cat stared at me accusingly, then shadowed me as I searched for the door to the attic. The next one I opened was to the bathroom, a clean but old-fashioned setup with a claw-foot bathtub and no shower. I noticed the claws because my mother loved them, had always wanted a bathtub like that. I thought they were creepy with knuckles and nails that might move if I stared long enough. I swallowed the thought, tore my eyes away.

Poised on the side of the tub, a soap dish held a bar with a flower carved into it, like it had not yet been used. There was also a blue glass bottle marked 'rose water' that lay beside it, its cork not quite in place. Slippers sat barren by the door, waiting for feet, and a granny bathrobe hung from a hook on the far wall.

The cat brushed my legs, urging me on, then reached up to stretch, its claws digging into my jeans. I moved just before he drew blood, resisted the urge to kick him.

Little demon, I muttered under my breath.

Heading back down the hall, I passed a table draped in a doily that reminded me of my grandmother's house... or at least the pictures I'd seen of it. She died when I was four, so memories of her were fleeting. Two unlit candles stood tall, like soldiers, guarding the dish that sat between them. It was a clear glass, thick and heavy, and held an assortment of candies. There were red and green balls enclosed in clear plastic, and yellow disks in gold wrappers. I selected one that looked like the sun, unwrapped it, and popped it into my mouth. Butterscotch. *Gross.* I spit it out into the wrapper and placed it back into the bowl.

Lazarus meowed as if to chide me.

"Shut up," I said, and moved toward the next door on the left. The knife in my head stabbed—punishment for a bad attitude.

The stairs that lay beyond were steeper than the last set. The air that wafted out was dusty and stagnant. I could only imagine what things contributed to the unique smell—moldy wallpaper, old books, decaying rodents, all things creepy-crawly. I fumbled to find the light switch and remembered the electricity was out, rolled my eyes at myself for being stupid.

I backtracked to the candy table and took one of the candlesticks, hunted through my pocket to find my lighter—the only piece I had left of my Dad. The silver top leaned back gracefully and, like I'd seen him do so many times, I brought the flame to life with a flick of my thumb. The smell was familiar and brought with it his face, then it backed away into the dark, into my memory. I swallowed the lump in my throat and stood tall, determined to be brave like he would expect me to be.

Holding the candle out like a torch, I climbed the stairs, the air becoming colder and thicker as I went. Lazarus stuck by my feet, not trusting me, but not confident about this exploration either.

See, Dad, I can do this. Even without you.

The stairwell walls were lined with thin wooden planks, textured like someone had taken great care to lay them neatly, but warped with time. As I crested the top stair, the candlelight spilled out into the room, reached up to the peaked ceiling that loomed above me, dissipated into the rafters. A shudder crept over my shoulder, and I fought the urge to run back down the stairs. I gritted my teeth, sucked in a breath.

I wouldn't let my Dad down; I was his brave girl.

The patter of the rain grew stronger, its rhythm beating down on the roof over my head. Lightning threw a glow through the windows on either side of the rectangular attic. The thunder boomed shortly after, vibrated the air around me. I was thankful for the candle, casting a glow on dust particles that floated through the air. They danced like fairies, confetti in celebration of a new guest.

Something had been waiting for me.

White sheets clung to large objects—likely furniture but could be treasure chests or secret closets to other worlds. I weaved among them, interested by the knick-knacks that lay scattered about the old wooden shelves. One for cooking with solid-looking skillets, a rolling pin, and an open recipe box, a hand-written card poking out of the top. Another for photographs in the midst of being filed into albums, and another for what looked like sewing materials. This must be where the needles and yarn were stored.

The candlelight fell on the pair, gleaming white spikes, maybe ivory. I pictured the elephant from which they were plucked, running around Africa toothless. I hung my head in shame for the old woman—a thief of nature. My social studies teacher, Mrs. Latham, would be horrified. I thought of her wildlife rights posters, pictures she showed us of her protesting animal testing in college.

This old woman must be evil.

I imagined the needles were ice picks, pursed my lips as I considered jabbing them into Mrs. Miller's eye socket. If I was a wicked girl, that's what I'd do.

I'd whisper, "Is this how young ladies are supposed to behave?" then stab, stab, stab. Of course, no one would believe a child would do such a thing. Especially if I said a crazy man had broken into the home when the electricity was out and attacked us. And secretly, it would be an elephant's revenge.

Who would tell on me, the cat?

Lazarus meowed as if he sensed my thoughts. No, he was not that clever. I ignored him, grabbing the stolen teeth and a ball of gray yarn, which I hoped wasn't spun from puppy fur. My stomach threatened to spill over as I thought of the tusks in my hands, but I choked down the nausea and focused on the sound of the rain. I was in no hurry to rejoin the old witch, so I lingered, searching the dimly lit attic for treasures.

I moved through the aisles of boxes, dust covers, and discarded wall hangings like a shopper in a department store. There were ceramic knick-knacks, a tarnished silver tea pot, and a collection of small records in faded paper covers. I remembered my cousin mentioning people paid a lot of money for old records, though I didn't know why. As I turned the corner, I stared for a moment, catching a figure out of the corner of my eye.

An old wedding gown hung on a styling mannequin, yellowed in some places, torn in others, frozen in time and waiting for a seamstress to mend. It was ghostly, an image of what Mrs. Miller had once been. Taller, thinner around the middle, perhaps elegant, though that was hard to imagine. Her body now was birdlike, a ball of a woman up top with skinny legs poking out from her housedress. My mind went back to the sagging skin that looped her ankles and I grimaced.

As I approached the corner haunted by the bride, the dress seemed to shift under my gaze, echoing a breeze from the rafters. Its satin was soft, lined with delicate lace meant to provide modesty. The bust line met the lace just in time to hide cleavage, and the frill traveled up an imaginary neck like a noose. What had once been white, or off-white, or eggshell, was now five shades of yellow in various places. I followed the train behind the silhouette, where the smell of cat urine wafted up from where Lazarus squatted. The giggle escaped through my nose as a snort.

Maybe he wasn't Mrs. Miller's confidante after all.

"Nice," I hissed, and his green eyes peered back, haughty.

"So, that's the game," I whispered, suddenly fond of this mischievous cat. "Let's raise the stakes."

The china set was delicate, an artist's paintbrush on a white backdrop. The pale blue flowers were exotic, lined with gold and rimmed with indigo.

"Perfect," I whispered, cocked an eyebrow and tossed a glance at the cat, my captive audience. I hesitated for a moment.

Would she hear?

No, that old lady was almost deaf. Besides, anyone selfish enough to steal animal parts and foolish enough to leave fine china laying about was just asking for trouble.

She deserved it.

"Back in my day, young ladies wore dresses." My voice croaked out of my throat, ugly and poisonous, mimicking hers. I lifted the plate above my head and let it fall. It met the floor with protest and splintered into pieces.

I shrugged my shoulders. "Ooopsie."

I grabbed a saucer this time, wound up my pitch.

"Back in my day, young ladies used manners," I spat, then tossed it at the wall behind the dress like a frisbee.

Crash.

"I'll show you what you can do with your tea." I grasped the dainty handle of the teacup, pulled my arm back, and let it fly, waiting for the satisfying shatter. But none came.

It bounced off the wall intact and landed behind a wardrobe whose door hung sadly on one hinge. Determined to see it through, I climbed over boxes, bookshelves, and errant pillows, then peeked behind the wardrobe to find the cup resting on an old quilt. But as I made my way around the final bend, something caught my attention on the other side of the attic.

At first, I thought it was Lazarus, investigating the treasures or chasing a frightened mouse. But he brushed against my leg, and I realized it couldn't have been him. So, what had cast the shadow? Something had passed before the round window, which now let in faded light in the storm's wake.

I strained my ears to hear, turned around the attic to catch any movement. My breath was loud in my ears. My heartbeat began to drum, head pulsing.

I was not alone.

"Mrs. Miller?" I said, hesitantly.

Nothing. Thunder rumbled in the distance like a response.

Terror filled my belly. It made my blood hot, skin cold, teeth clench. My breath came fast. If I stood still, I didn't know what would come. If I moved, it might see me.

Lazarus' growl was all I needed to get moving. I jumped back over the boxes, tumbling them in random directions, legs moving faster than the rest of me. I shot down the stairs, the nausea kicking in. Behind me I could hear it.

Someone was breathing.

As I stumbled down the stairs, I missed one, then another, then I plunged into darkness. My face hit the door with a thud and the candlelight that remained back up in the attic went out. All that guided me was the soft glow creeping in through the windows upstairs, reflecting onto the attic eaves.

"Help!" I screamed, grabbing for the handle. "Let me out!"

My voice grew more desperate. The air, cold and clammy around me, seeped into my hair, my mouth, my soul.

My voice went up an octave, "Help!" Then the words dissipated into feral cries as I grasped for the door handle, its knob turning over and over again, not catching. I pounded, used my shoulder, kicked. And then turned the knob the other way.

I spilled out into the hallway, now lit by the other candle on the table with the candy. Relief flooded into my body and I sprang up, swung the door shut just as Lazarus leapt to safety. I backed away from the door, not wanting to turn my back, not trusting what was on the other side.

The stabbing pain returned, a headache to punish the guilty.

It was embarrassing to recall—what I'd just done. Panicked. Let my imagination get the best of me. I was even good sport enough to laugh at myself, but thankful that no one had witnessed the scene. The realization that Dad would be disappointed floated in, then out of my awareness. I heard his voice in my mind: *You shouldn't have broken the china. You should apologize.*

And you shouldn't have left, I muttered under my breath, to the ghost of Dad who was my constant companion.

In my distraction, I backed up all the way into another room. The door creaked open slowly, its hinges protesting all the way. The windows were covered in a sheer fabric draped to the floor, the only light outside filtered through a stormy sky. It smelled of baby powder—a scent of childhood that brought with it images of my mother and feelings of safety.

It was a strong contrast to what I'd just escaped.

Reluctant to rejoin Mrs. Miller and curious about the baby powder room, I lifted the other candle from its guard beside the butterscotch disks. The light revealed a girl's room, decorated in pink and lace and filled with old-fashioned toys. This bed had a canopy, too, but not like the one in the other room. This one had frills and ribbons climbing up the posts, and a delicate footstool meant to boost a child into the sea of pillows.

There was a bookcase with hard-cover fairy tale books. I pulled out the copy of *Hansel & Gretel*, wondered at the elaborate illustrations, noticed how much Mrs. Miller looked like the witch luring children.

There was a jewelry box on the bookcase as well; when I lifted the top, a ballerina spun round, with a soft tinkling of a familiar tune. *The Nutcracker,* I thought, recalling my Mom's favorite ballet she dragged me to last year. There were lockets and trinkets inside the box, not cracker jack prizes, but engraved necklaces and what looked like a diamond bracelet. This was a spoiled child, I thought, if stuck in another century.

I moved to the corner nook, where toys sat as if in mid-play. A tower of wooden blocks was piled high, like it was in the process of becoming something... a castle perhaps. A circle of marbles and a collection of jacks, neither of which I knew how to play. A silver slinky, silent and bored, resting on its side. And a table set up for a tea party with tiny plates and cups ready for entertaining. The saucers had M&Ms on them and I grabbed a selection, popped them in my mouth.

It was then that I noticed the doll, sitting as a lonely guest at the table. She was unlike any doll I'd ever seen, about the size of a toddler. Her blonde hair was in ringlets, her eyes wide open with what looked like real lashes. Her dress was ancient—something out of *Little House on the Prairie*, I guessed—bratty Nellie, not farmgirl Laura. She sat in a black miniature rocking chair, a frozen look of delight on her face. The bib around her neck said "Eleanor."

The more I looked at her, the more she seemed to look back at me.

I backed away, not wanting to disturb this place, this museum. But as I turned to exit, the light from the candle reflected in a mirror, grayed out with age, but still hanging proudly. It was enclosed in a gold frame, elaborate with flourishes and faces, disappearing into one another. The surface was tarnished, I could only imagine from time. Maybe mirrors were made differently back in the day—in whatever century birthed Mrs.

Miller. There were silver and gold streaks that seemed to climb through the surface, making my reflection hazy. I moved closer, the flame dancing, tossing shadows behind the frame and onto the wall. The light played tricks on my eyes, making the faces swim and claws appear from the decoration.

This was something that belonged to a princess. She'd sit on her high bed of pillows with her ringlets like gold, her grandmother bringing her chamomile tea and cinnamon toast, her father coming home to kiss her on her forehead.

Princesses always had fathers.

The mirror was a dream, pulling me in, lulling me to sleep. The girl who stared back at me looked foreign, her eyes larger than mine, bluer, darker.

And then she smiled.

But I wasn't smiling.

I gasped, dropped the candle, ran out the door as fast as I could move. Lazarus bounded down the stairs beside me, hissing.

Mrs. Miller stood at the bottom of the stairs, arms crossed, her face like stone. Despite my fear, I was so taken aback by her expression that I froze in mid-step, hand on the railing, mouth wide open.

"I see you met my granddaughter," she said, sternly.

The realization washed over me in a cold sweat.

"Eleanor, what did I say about little girls? They are polite. They don't bother guests." Her face shifted from anger into something else. Something... worried. It was then that the smell of burning reached my nose.

"Eleanor, what did you do?" Mrs. Miller shrieked as she pushed past me and up the stairs. "What a bad little girl!" she shouted.

It was the last thing I heard before running out the front door.

This piece originally appeared in *Coffin Bell Journal*, vol. 3, no. 2, 2020.

The Game

"You don't understand anything, Mom! You don't *know*!"

This was the last thing I heard before Sammie slammed the door in my face—for the third time that week. I swallowed the lump in my throat, placed my hand on the door tenderly, like it might melt the ice between us somehow. The wood beneath the glossy paint that had chipped away was solid, dependable, thick.

And still closed.

The hand that lingered there was so much older than I'd remembered. Blue veins pulsed beneath aging pink skin, a spot of brown beginning to form in the space between two bones. It was my own fault for tanning all those summers, back when it was "cool." A memory of laughter ebbed in, splashing water, late night talks, friendship that was impossible to find now in my forties. Of course, it wasn't always sweet. I shuddered. The nostalgia went just as quickly as it had come, no longer in my grasp.

How did I get here? Middle-aged. Single mom. Saying the same shit my mother said to me when I was a teen. The stuff you swear you'll never say. And my Sammie, my baby girl, hating me for it. It was more painful than I'd imagined. Silently apologizing to my Mom, I turned and walked back down the hall to my coffee. I knew better than to pursue this conversation right now, when she was feeling reckless.

I passed the framed pictures on the wall, black and whites that tracked Sammie's growth over time. I ignored the thin layer of dust that clung to the bottom lip of the frames, my gaze drawn to her sweet green eyes. Dark lashes framed them like tendrils, reaching out into the world, further from me the older she got.

I paused by the most recent photo, where she wasn't even smiling. "I don't want to show my teeth," she'd decided. "Dawn says the gap in front makes me look like an idiot."

I'd wanted to reach through her cell phone and smack that nasty little girl who delighted in taking pokes at my daughter. And I knew the comments were far worse than she'd confessed. Despite my anger, I'd merely said, "Dawn can't decide what you should look like. That's up to you. Don't give away your power."

She'd given me the stare of death in response, her eyes turning olive with bitterness, staring down the barrel of her cute pug nose.

I'd gritted my teeth. I'd sighed and counted to twenty. I'd strangled the voice of the younger me that wanted to scream at the top of my lungs: "Dawn is a bitch who is using you! And when she's done all that will be left are pieces I will have to pick up!" But the wiser part of me, the one who remembered the aftermath of such "friendships," knew that she was going to have to learn this lesson the hard way.

As I sat down at the kitchen table and wrapped my aging hands around the barely warm coffee mug, I whispered a prayer that Sammie might escape her teens with fewer scars than I had. I wished that she might focus on the friends who actually gave a shit about her—the ones she often cast aside when the cooler kids came around.

I peered down into the cup, examining the ring of creamer dust that hadn't quite made it into the hazelnut liquid. The large eyes that looked back at me were afraid.

Because she was wrong.

Because I *did* know.

*

Fall, 1990

I sat in the back seat of Marjorie Mason's white jeep, pretending the air streaming through the open roof wasn't too cold. It slapped my face, licking my hair to one side and then the other, as we barreled down the highway at 70 miles an hour. Marjorie was swerving a little, evidence of the wine coolers we'd had before leaving her Parkside mansion, but I wasn't worried. Two weeks ago, I couldn't have imagined being included on this adventure. It was going to be a night filled with magic.

Sandwiched between Brit Chambers and Chloe Sims, I imagined my body soaking up some of their glamour. My gaze fell on our legs, six thighs neatly lined up together, but two of these things were not like the others. To my left, Brit's tan skin peaked through the rips in her sand blasted jeans. She was an athlete and I could imagine the finely shaped muscles underneath. To my right, Chloe's long, thin legs looked sleek

in tight stirrup leggings. Their remarkable length was what had
won her a modeling contract in the Sears catalog.

Then my eyes fell on my own shorter, wider thighs, hiding
beneath baggy Girbaud jeans. The ends had been French
cuffed, but earlier Marjorie had looked me up and down,
demanded an immediate change if she "were to be seen with
me" tonight. I'd complied before she'd finished the sentence.
Her eyes fell on me now, a reflection in the rear-view mirror,
her blue eyes lined with black like an Egyptian princess. They
turned up as she smiled but looked more mischievous than
friendly. As her gaze returned to the road, her blonde hair
whipped back and forth in the wind, like a horse's mane.

Kristen Grant, who rode shotgun, turned around then, stared
at me openly. All these girls were intimidating, but she was the
only one who really scared me. Her naturally ebony hair had
been dyed even darker—a blue black that made her white skin
pallid. Her lips were coated in thick red, her murky gray eyes
haunting and bare. A cigarette dangled from her hand; she
held it low so the wind wouldn't sweep it away. She cocked
her head to the side, watching me. I attempted a smile, but she
did not match it. As she drew the cigarette closer to my knee,
her eyes remained locked on my face.

"Kristen!" said Chloe beside me, putting up her hands in a
"stop" motion.

Drawing the glowing tip away from me, she looked up, raised
one eyebrow. "What?"

"That's not necessary," replied Chloe, raising her voice above
the wind.

"I just wanted to see how far she was willing to go."

A shiver ran through my body as Kristen turned back around, and for the first time that night, I started to wonder why they'd brought me along if she didn't approve. And clearly she didn't. I could almost see the steam coming off her, angry at Chloe's intervention. It was not in line with the group's pecking order.

Like a pack of wild dogs, every group had their Alpha and Beta. Marjorie was the Alpha. She drove the car. She called the shots. She had final say. But Kristen was the Beta, second only to Marjorie, and she had probably fought for that position. It was an unspoken rule that teenage girls just knew, even if they didn't have labels.

Never fuck with the head bitches in charge unless you want their wrath.

As if she could sense my anxiety, Chloe smiled reassuringly, her green eyes alluring and gentle. Even after she looked away, returned her gaze to the window and the world that flashed by, I examined her profile. Her pink lips were glossed and rested in a seductive pout that I had tried to mimic in the mirror at home. I imagined how it might feel to pose for the camera, tossing a doe-eyed glance toward the shutter, peeking out from beneath shaggy auburn bangs. I fantasized about waking up in the morning in a body that was lithe and graceful, with no roll that paunched out when I laid on my side.

To my left, Brit made a joke about Marjorie's weaving into the other lane and we all chuckled. Even Chloe's laughter sounded like bells in comparison to my awkward guffaw. Her elegance was effortless. And while Brit was not perhaps the most poised, she was strong and toned, kissed by the sun. Her dark blonde hair was streaked with pale strands that framed her face and despite her lack of makeup, her brown eyes were deep pools of chocolate—the kind you'd see on a yellow lab—that drew you in with charm. Her expressive eyebrows sat guard like mischievous elves. She was the kind of girl that put the "sexy" into the schoolgirl uniform.

Feeling eyes on me, I glanced up at the rearview mirror again, where I found Marjorie's black-lined irises examining me under a microscope. They flicked to the road, then back to me, dangerously playful.

"So, Molly, I'm curious, just how far would you go to be one of us?" Marjorie said.

The question hung in the air like a guillotine, ready to slice off my head. Kristen peered around the shotgun seat, tossed Chloe a glare like darts. Speech eluded me. I didn't know what to say because I wasn't sure myself.

"I don't know." It escaped my mouth before I gave it permission. As soon as the words left, I wanted to cram them back in, but they were no longer mine. They had become group property.

"You don't know?" Marjorie sang back to me, sweetly but not sincerely. "Then why are we wasting our time with you?"

"You're not," I spat quickly. "I'll do whatever it takes."

My newfound courage was more than an answer; it was a declaration, even to myself. After all, what could they ask me to do that would be that bad?

*

The five of us stood in darkness, at the gates of the old abandoned amusement park, its signs battered, worn, faded from sunlight and too many winters of neglect. Weeds grew up from cracks in the cement that had once been a clean path to joy. I could almost hear children's laughter, smell cotton candy and elephant ears, feel the excitement that always built in my stomach the night before a trip to ride rollercoasters. I'd never been to a defunct park before. There was something crushing about standing at its lonely ticket booth, the turnstile frozen in time.

We stood side by side, staring into the ghost town bathed in moonlight. I turned my head, peered down the row of silhouettes, not sure what to expect. Marjorie turned suddenly, stepped before us as if she was on a stage.

"Ladies, our adventure begins here," she said, sweeping her long blonde hair to the side. "Prepare yourselves for a journey that will surpass all those that have come before."

In silence, we followed her—pecking order clear. Marjorie led us through the jungle of broken rides, with Kristen right behind, leaving a trail of cigarette ash. Chloe was next, eyeing the frozen merry-go-round, her breath escaping plump lips in smoke. Next was Brit, athletic like a lynx, nimble among the rusting metal that surrounded us. She stopped to aim a ball at a clown's wooden mouth in the shape of an 'o', hit her target effortlessly. Dancing to music only she could hear, she looked at me triumphantly, shook off her victory as she rejoined the line. And then there was me, unsure of my steps, creeped out by darkness, bringing up the tail. They wouldn't even notice if I got lost.

We wove through the aging trail, the ghosts of rollercoasters rushing past, the echoes of thrilled screams breathing over our shoulders. The breeze picked up as we passed the swing ride, the empty seats creaking on their chains. The buckets on the ferris wheel hung still, the giant teacups no longer spun, the water for the log rides had long dried up.

Marjorie brought us to a stop at the Big Hill, a wooden rollercoaster known for its initial high drop-off and series of smaller hills that gave kids the belly-flops, once upon a time.

"Here we are," she said, sweeping her hand across the scene as if to introduce it. "The game tonight, ladies, is drunk coaster climbing."

"That's badass," said Kristen. "I should know, it was my idea." She looked at the rest of us as if we were her subjects, her shadowy hair like a cowl around her pale face.

"Our idea," said Marjorie, irritated. She spat the words at Kristen like poison. "I brought you here, remember?"

"Course, Marj—our idea," Kristen shrugged, but lifted her red lip in a mock growl when Marjorie turned her back.

"The flavor of the evening," continued Marjorie, as she dragged a crate from the side of the trail, "is peppermint schnapps." She lifted the bottle out of the crate along with five paper cups.

"Wait, but—" began Brit, twisting her sun-kissed hair nervously.

"But nothing." Marjorie cut her off, glared at her. "It's not my problem that you got so drunk off this at that frat party that you puked your guts up. Suck it up, Brit. Or have you lost your edge?"

Brit swallowed hard. "No. I'm good."

"Chloe, any objections?" Marjorie eyed her coolly.

Chloe's glossed lips pursed, relaxed into a smile. "The mintier the better," she replied.

Marjorie was appeased. "That's what I like to hear."

Kristen's eyes fell on me. "What about that one?" she said to Marjorie, who shrugged.

"She can stay if she can keep up."

Peppermint schnapps. I think I'd stolen a sip or two from my mother's hot chocolate spiked with the stuff, but had never had it straight from the bottle. This was do or die.

"No problem," I said, even convincing myself. The first sip was the worst. The liquid burned as it went down my throat, leaving a trail of mint that seeped up through my nose.

"Tell us something interesting about *you*, Molly," said Marjorie, lighting up a cigarette that she took from Kristen's pack. She didn't bother to ask permission.

"Yeah, we don't keep secrets in this group," said Chloe.

"We just keep them from everyone else," added Kristen.

Brit nodded in agreement.

My mind swam. We had finished the bottle when Marjorie pulled a second one from the crate. *Something interesting, something interesting...*

"I can tie a cherry stem in a knot with my tongue," I offered.

"The guys will love that," said Brit.

"You'll need a make-over," said Marjorie, "If you're going to hang with us."

"A major one," whispered Kristen under her breath.

"I'll do it," offered Chloe, whose eyes flicked to mine. "I mean, if you want me to."

"I want you to." Marjorie rolled her eyes. "Like, tomorrow."

The blood rushed to my face and I was glad for the darkness. Drink. Drink. Drink. Yes, a make-over sounded great. I wondered if Chloe had a magic wand that could make me thinner, taller—better.

The second bottle was now halfway gone and I felt like I was floating. I looked at Brit beside me, who was very quiet. I imagined she was choking down nausea. I hoped I wasn't too close behind her.

"Oh, my god, this girl's actually funny," Kristen said, moving toward me. She put her hand on my knee like an initiation. I couldn't even remember what I'd said, but everyone else loved it.

I was *in*.

When I stood up, the world moved. Chloe grabbed one of my arms and Brit the other. We were going to do this together.

"Drunk coaster climbing!" yelled Kristen. Her voice echoed through the empty park, bouncing off the abandoned mineshaft ride and crumbling bumper car stadium.

"Woohoo!" we screamed, our voices blending.

The roller coaster track stretched upward like a curvy ladder, the steps further apart the closer we got to them. We scaled one of the smaller mountains carefully, pecking order preserved. We were like ants on the back of a dragon, reaching towards its angry head. The moon hung above us, a spotlight on a dark blanket. If only the rest of the school could see me now.

I was one of them.

I was flying high.

"Molly! Truth or dare?" yelled Marjorie. Her voice crawled down the ladder toward me. I loved hearing her say my name. I was her friend now.

"Truth!" I yelled back, clutched the next ladder rung in my hand, pulled myself up.

"Have you lost your V-card yet?"

"No lies!" yelled Kristen. "Remember, we keep the secrets between us."

I swallowed, climbed.

"No!"

I waited for the judgement, but it never came.

"We'll have to fix that," responded Brit, laughing into the night air. I laughed back.

"Your turn, Molly!" shouted Kristen. "You ask!"

Next rung up. The others were moving faster than me. I picked up the pace.

"Chloe, truth or dare?" I shouted.

"Truth!"

What would impress them? What could I ask?

"Is Brad as good in the sack as everyone says?"

"I wouldn't know!" she yelled back, pulling herself up onto the ledge. She peered down at me, her eyes widened, probably from taking in the height. I was afraid to look back, so I stayed focused on her.

I was there—I was one of them!

I tossed my fear aside, pulled myself up the final rung onto the landing.

"What do you mean you wouldn't know?" I said between breaths. "Aren't you two dating?"

"I haven't lost my V-card either," she said, giving me a soft smile. Maybe we're more alike than I thought. I smiled back.

"Wow, this is a serious view," Chloe said. I followed her gaze, out over the sprawling cemetery before us. As far as I could see, there were obsolete rides, worn out toys whose skeletal bodies stood frozen, decaying slowly in the weather. They glowed in the moonlight, their stillness unsettling. Something groaned among the corpses, the objection disappearing into the wind.

"Your turn, Chloe," said Kristen, poking her in the arm.

Chloe licked her lips, paused.

"Marjorie, truth or dare?"

Marjorie turned to face us, something dangerous in her eyes.

"Dare."

Chloe was caught off guard.

"Well, we're already drunk climbing a roller coaster, so, I don't know if I can top that." She thought, put her finger to her lips, looked around. "I dare you to jump to that ledge." She was desperate—the next ledge was pretty far.

She reconsidered.

"But if you don't want to, it's ok, we'll just do a truth."

"No, no," said Marjorie. "This girl never turns down a dare."

She stared at the distance between the two platforms, one for the hill we were on, the other made for a coaster going in the opposite direction. Maybe they were there for maintenance, maybe just for emergencies—if a car ever got stuck mid-ride.

"Marjie, I only said it as a joke," said Chloe, nervously. "There's no way that's a good idea."

"Puh-lease," she said. "Are you saying I can't do it?"

"No, I'm saying you *shouldn't* do it." Chloe's eyes grew wider and my own mirrored hers. The nerves tickled my stomach, teased the contents that sloshed back and forth inside me.

"Who are you, my mom? Just shut up and move back."

Kristen stepped forward, "Hey, Marj, no one doubts you can do it. But maybe it's not a good idea since you've been drinking."

Marjorie put up her hand and made a hissing noise. "Shhhhhh. Shut it." The girls fell silent. I held my breath, looked down along the ladder we had climbed. My head spun. We were up three, four stories maybe.

Marjorie moved to the edge of the platform, leaned against the railing, took a running start, leapt toward the other ledge. My breath caught in my throat. Her blonde hair trailed after her like a cape. She was supergirl. She landed hard, collapsed onto her side, finally safe. She released a triumphant scream that wound through the park like a banshee.

With a sigh of relief, I sat down on the platform. My stomach threatened to explode.

"I can't believe you just fucking did that," said Brit. She plopped down next to me and I felt power in her company. I put my hand on her back, comforting her. She leaned in, put her head on my shoulder. This was what friends did, supported each other.

Marjorie grinned, her white teeth reflecting the moonlight. "I know, right? I'm so impressive." She slowly outstretched her arm, pointed at Kristen. "Ok, girlfriend, don't let me down. Kristen, truth or dare? Don't you fucking say truth."

Kristen raised her head high, hovered above Marjorie's challenge.

"Dare," she hissed. I couldn't tell if she was pissed or enthralled.

"Join me," said Marjorie, sweetly, cocking her head to one side like a golden retriever. With her pointer finger, she made a "come hither" gesture.

I closed my eyes, the anxiety rising in my bones. My teeth started to chatter. This was getting to be too much. This was... stupid.

"Kristen, don't do it," said Brit, looking up at her.

Chloe put her hand on Kristen's arm, who just shook it off. "Back off, bitches, I'm up for it."

"Oh my god," Brit murmured, buried her head in my shoulder even further.

Kristen backed up, following Marjorie's lead. With three steps as a running start, she dove, shrieked as she leapt toward the other ledge. Her feet touched down, but only partially on the platform. She wobbled backwards, waved her arms around in panic to catch her balance.

I froze. Chloe gasped. Brit screamed. And Marjorie grabbed her sleeve, ripping her black leather jacket, but it was enough to sway her forward. She crumpled to her knees, clumsily.

"Holy shit," Kristen muttered. "Holy shit!" she screamed, her eyes as wide around as the clown's on the tattered billboard behind her.

"You've only got eight more lives left, sister," said Marjorie, coolly. They slapped hands, giving five. "You're the only one badass enough to follow my lead."

"Or stupid enough," mumbled Brit, under her breath. I looked up to see if anyone else had heard.

"What was that, Brit?" said Marjorie, her head cocked to one side. "You got somethin' to say?"

"Yeah, I think we should get down," Brit responded, pulling her head upright, not backing down from Marjorie's glare.

"Oh, yeah? Well we're not done. Truth or dare?" Marjorie's blonde hair reflected the moonlight eerily, hay on a scarecrow's head.

Brit rolled her eyes in annoyance.

"It's not your turn, Marjorie, it's Kristen's," she said.

"Yeah, well, I just saved her life so she owes me one." Marjorie was amped up. Maybe it was the adrenaline rush from the jump. "So? Truth or dare?"

Brit shook her head, shrugged. "Truth."

"Did you or did you not sleep with Michael?" Marjorie's question flew from one ledge to the other, knocked the wind out of Brit. I could see it on her face, felt her body stiffen next to me.

"Wish ya woulda picked dare, huh?" Marjorie's sweet tone was a lure.

Brit stared back at her dumbly. "I don't..." she started, but her voice trailed off. Her brown eyes were round like a puppy's, sweet to a fault. She looked over to Chloe, whose jaw hung open. She finally took a seat beside us, surrendering to the inquisition.

"It's ok, it's not really a question," said Kristen. "We already know you're a whore who sleeps with other peoples' boyfriends."

I was afraid to move, caught in the spell that was unfolding around me. I could see Brit's lower lip quivering, her eyes searching for answers in the night air.

"So, you can't even answer a simple question," said Marjorie, her words spreading the sweet butter, making room for the knives. "I guess that makes you stupid, too."

"Marj—." Chloe started to speak but Marjorie would have none of it.

"Shut up. You're not innocent either, little miss narcissist. You knew about this."

Chloe shook her head, her auburn hair like fringe around her cupid face.

"How did you—."

"I said, shut up!" Marjorie yelled. "Or do I have to spell it out for you?" She turned to Kristen. "God, how have we put up with this idiocy for so long?"

Kristen just shook her head, looked down her nose, across the synapse at the two girls beside me. I was invisible.

"So, you can't deal with 'truth', let's see about 'dare'." Marjorie and Kristen locked eyes, their mouths twisted up into grins—two jokers in a deck of cards.

"They're pretty hot, Marjie, aren't they?" Kristen drew out her words and they dripped with sarcasm.

"So hot." Marjorie pulled a zippo out of her pocked, played with the top, back and forth, back and forth. "The name of the game tonight, ladies, is drunk coaster climbing. *Hot*, drunk coaster climbing. Your challenge is to make it to the ground before I light this bitch on fire."

My heart leapt, started pounding in my chest. "Is this real?" I whispered. "This is a joke, right?" I looked at Brit, whose eyes were leaking tears. I searched Chloe's face, who looked back at Marjorie in disbelief.

"Cut it out, Marjie," she said. "You're scaring Molly."

"Who? Oh, yeah, the fat tagalong." She huffed, dismissing the idea of *me* entirely. "Well, you know we had to have a reason to come out here, so she's really just an unfortunate casualty," she responded, perched on the landing like a crow, teasing the space between us like she owned it. Like she owned *us*.

"This is boring me, Marjie," said Kristen, examining her fingernails. They were black shellac in the misty night. "Can we get on with it already?"

Marjorie shrugged, nodded. "Sure, sorry."

She transformed from angelic deity into vengeful hag, pointed at Chloe.

"You're a bitch."

Her finger moved to Brit.

"You're a whore."

And her gaze finally rested on me.

"And you're a nobody, so no one will miss you anyway." Her body leaned back toward Kristen, her voice softened. "Better?"

"Fabulous," Kristen growled, looked at us out of the corner of her eye. "Ready, set, go."

Like cats, Marjorie and Kristen jumped into action, began scrambling down their side of the coaster, which was already a little closer to the ground. My body was in motion before my mind could catch up, racing back down the coaster the way I had come up. Brit and Chloe followed my lead, the threat of dissolving into a burning pyre shoving us into partial sobriety. Either Marjorie had a warped sense of humor or she really planned to burn us to the ground. She had called me a nobody—said no one would miss me.

She was a *bitch*.

My body shook as I moved, legs reaching for the next step, hands clutching tight to the rung above. My heart was a drum in my chest, the nausea rising from my stomach in waves. Leg, other leg, hand, other hand. Faster and faster I climbed downward, my eyes flicking from the rollercoaster under me to the shadows that crept down the other hill.

They were ahead of us, but not by much.

I was halfway down when I heard the crack, followed by a scream. My eyes flew to the other hill, where I saw blonde hair weaving back and forth in the moonlight, legs dangling from a broken step.

"Help!" she screamed. "Kristen!"

"Oh, my god, Marjorie!" Kristen's voice wove through the massive wooden coaster frame, between support beams, right to my ears. "Hold on, I'm coming!"

I faltered as a gust of wind pushed my body away from the coaster. I hugged the wooden frame tight, preferring bruises to the broken bones that would come with letting go. Gulping, I refocused and resumed the descent, trying to block out the shrieks that were becoming more desperate. I was suddenly aware of the aging wood that supported me—supported all of us. We were intruding on a burial ground and it finally occurred to me that there might be a price for trespassing.

My feet hit the ground with a thud and so did Marjorie's body.

*

A knock on the door pulled me out of the memory's web, back through the alleys of decrepit rides, past the bumper cars, away from the laughing clown posters, till only the scent of cotton candy lingered. My grip on the coffee cup relaxed and the circulation returned to my aging fingers as I opened the front door.

Dawn stood on the front stoop, high heeled boots hiked above her knees, short-shorts barley long enough to cover her rear, and nothing but naked thighs in between. Her face was airbrushed, made up like the cover of Cosmo, hiding the essence of who she really was on the inside. The cowboy hat on her head was on backwards, but she didn't know that. And I wasn't going to tell her.

"Hi, Sammie's Mom," she said with sugary sweetness but no smile. "Is she ready?"

Sammie appeared beside me, saving me from what I really wanted to say.

"I'll be out in a sec, ok?" she said.

Dawn nodded, raised one eyebrow at me in triumph, walked toward the car with one butt cheek peeking out.

"Mom, I'm sorry I yelled before," she said, softly. Her green eyes held mine and I could still see the child in her, even beneath the eyeliner and mascara. "But you've got to chill. I'm almost seventeen. Seriously."

She leaned forward, hugged me briefly.

"Love you," she said.

"Love you," I echoed, eating my other thoughts: *be careful, don't trust her, don't go drunk coaster climbing.*

Sammie climbed into the shotgun seat, the beta to the alpha. As the car pulled away, I could only see the outline of Dawn's middle finger held up in the rearview mirror at me.

 This piece originally appeared in *Obra/Artifact*, 2019.

Selkie Skin

Ohio, U.S.A., 1944.

It was late September when the fog rolled into Fairport
Harbor, hugging the shores of Lake Erie in mist. It awoke
something in Elizabeth, even in the confines of her bedroom
on Prospect Street, where she became lost in the waves from
her window. Her eyes drifted from the graying evening to the
crumpled letter on her bed. She smoothed it out, finding the
words smeared from tears and marred by creases she couldn't
erase.

I'm not ready to be a father.

The ink slapped her. Fury burned beneath her skin and with it
came a great shame that washed over her face, flushing it red
and hot.

How could she have been so stupid? That's what Mother would say.
Mother, with her prim poise and judgmental stare that
haunted Elizabeth as she grew older. Each hint at her
blossoming womanhood was an offense. A quiet anger
seethed in her, buried beneath layers of compliance and the
desire for love.

Mother was a complicated word. An unpredictable mixture of
salt, bitter, and sweet. A bakery smell that lured her in but
rotted on her tongue.

There was nothing about Mother that cherished her. Perhaps there once had been, long before she could remember. But no more. And now she could add her first beau to the raw wound that was her heart. Perhaps she was just unlovable.

But no. Something inside her denied this. Sister Mary Catherine had cared for her once, even if it had been her duty at the orphanage. When Elizabeth was unwanted, the nun's arms had held her tight.

Love was possible.

Is possible.

Elizabeth's eyes returned to the windowpane, and beyond, through the fog for a beacon of hope. The lighthouse glowed in the distance, warning seamen of the break wall.

*

Elizabeth drew up the sash and climbed through the open window onto the porch roof. She shimmied down the trellis and landed on dew-covered grass. Her slippers threatened to slide, but she righted herself against the house, pausing to listen for stirring from within. Mother would have her hide if she saw.

The waves lapped the shore. Soupy haze hung in the air. A dog barked in the distance.

She was free.

Elizabeth crept across the street to the lakeshore, following its slope down, down to the place where it met the water. No sand here, just rocks and water. The pale glow of a distant moon fused the mist with silver, just enough to see.

The waves were otherworldly—dark shadows that waxed and waned. A field of wildflowers dancing in the breeze. A tornado of starlings against a pale sky. A blanket shaken between friends before it's folded. An invitation to a long slumber.

Mesmerized, Elizabeth drew the bottle out from her bathrobe pocket, its glass cool in her fingers. She turned it around and around in the faint light, remembering her scribbles on the rolled paper within. A prayer for grace. A dream of love. A cry for deliverance.

Take me away from here. Far, far away.

She took a deep breath and tossed the message in a bottle into the writhing waters, sending with it all her desires.

The bottle danced atop the waves and she imagined its journey to Michigan, or New York, or even Canada. But its mission was short-lived. The tide drew it back toward Elizabeth, trapping the message against the rocks, until it lodged in a crevice.

No. The word leaked out of her mouth.

She knelt where it was stuck, able to see it but not to reach it. With a long piece of driftwood in hand, she maneuvered it, prying and poking. She would not let her hope die on this shore.

And then it gave way. Her effort thrust it back out into the waters, taking with it her frustration. And her balance.

She teetered on the edge of the rocks—a pin top spinning, faster as she fell, colors blurring into paint strokes of cream and white and silver. And finally dissipating into a deep, deep blue.

*

Elizabeth sank into an abyss of choking and lights in the corners of her eyes—fairies come to steal her to another realm. Cold needled her body, wrapping her in an icy rhythm, back and forth, back and forth. A dangerous lullaby. Her arms flailed, her legs kicked, and she grasped for the edge that eluded her.

She broke to the surface and then was pulled down again. The waves were more ferocious than they had appeared. Not wildflowers, or starlings in flight, or a soft, warm blanket. No. They were angry jaws, open and chomping, drawing her toward an enormous belly where ships in rough waters go to die.

It was Sister Mary Catherine's soft voice that wafted in like smoke, dancing in turns and shimmers, lingering on the edges of Elizabeth's psyche, reaching out to save her. Just like she had in that dark time—the time when Mother had held her down in the bathtub.

Elizabeth blocked out the memory in the waking world, but here, under the veils of half-sleep where she walked on the edge of death, it stalked her.

Elizabeth sank down, down, into herself. To a time before.

Strong hands on her throat. Pushing her under the surface.
Gasping for breath. Slippery, so slippery. She wiggled away
and Mother fell—the crack of her skull against the tub echoed.
Scrambling out, sliding on the floor, to underneath her bed
where she hid for hours. Her cave, her safe space. Mother
wouldn't go where the spiders lurked.

Elizabeth struggled for breath between the currents. Her
insides had become water, thick with sludge and grime. The
wheezing, a vibration from deep within, clutching her from
the inside out.

*Sweet child, come with me to the Tuatha De Danann, to Tir Na Nog,
said Sister Mary Catherine. Where the children are fair, the music is
sweet, and the land is ever green.*

The rumble of a foghorn bellowed from above, sank down
beneath her and swam around her in ripples. Its throb was
thunder in the lake, waking things that had long slept. It was
the sound of her soul, a last cry for salvation.

Come child. Swim with the selkie, forever free and loved.

The blanket wrapped around her, warm like a mother's arms
should be. Fingers morphed into fins, whiskers sprouted from
her muzzle, and she slithered through the swells, dancing to
the tune of the lake. The base of the foghorn was a call from
her ancestors, halfway around the world.

Sing with me, child, said Sister Mary Catherine.

As she crested the waves, sounds emerged from deep within her belly, wild and raw. Barks, grunts, and tenor notes not meant for a human girl. Her eyes widened, revealing a world under the water's surface that glowed and shifted, teaming with life.

She was reborn.

She rode the ripples to the break wall, and through the breach to open waters, where the fog was thicker. The glow from the lighthouse dimmed in her wake, and with it went memory of her name. There was only the pull toward freedom.

*

The message in the bottle swept upon the shores of Fairport Harbor the next morning. The young girl who opened it knew not what to make of its message save that it sought release: *Far, far away.* And in the distance, in the pale silver hue that was left of the dissipating fog, she thought she saw a seal bobbing up and down in the waves, singing.

 This piece originally appeared in *Olit*, 2024.

Part Two: Mother

"Mothers are the keepers of secrets, the guardians of our darkest fears. They know us better than we know ourselves, and they'll do whatever it takes to protect us—even if it means facing their own demons."

~ Ajaz Ahmad Khawaja

The Ripper Society

Liverpool, England.

April, 1889.

My charming prince is the worst kind of lie, Florie thought, as she placed the key in the lock. If she proceeded with this betrayal, there would be no going back. She remembered the image of English luxury he had painted, then lured her into the bonds of marriage. And now here she was with two children and a beast.

Whatever lay on the other side of the door would answer her burning question: *What, exactly, had her husband been hiding?* If ever a discovery was to be made, it must be now. It would not be easy to secure the key again.

With a turn of her hand, the door released and she pushed it open. The heavy oak plank groaned on its hinges in a warning. But it was too late. She had stepped inside, despite the nerves that twisted her stomach.

The smell of pipe tobacco surrounded her and mingled with the liquor that flowed for the gentlemen the night prior. But this was no surprise, for she had heard their raucous laughter before she retired; it had continued to almost dawn. She lay her palms on the waistline of her dress and smoothed the fabric there, repeating the words that had given her courage over the last few hours: *I will no longer be made to look like a fool in my own home.*

She had overheard at least one suspect comment made by Mr. Francis Thompson. "Poor girl did not know how to handle me," he'd said. "Jim, I doubt you might inspire that kind of awe." *Was this a contest of carnal manipulation then?* She mused. *Did they sneak harlots in through the foyer after I retired?*

Her husband's library was like a cave, tucked under the stairs at Battlecrease House. The floor creaked as she crossed it, an orchestral piece for her comedy of errors. Or was it a tragedy? All would be revealed soon enough. She had but to retrace their movements of the night before and seek out evidence of deceit.

The circular oak table that had been part of her dowery was still littered with playing cards and empty Moser crystal glasses. There was even a silver snuff box, cast aside like garbage. She smiled to herself as she pocketed the trinket, like she had won something already. Then her eyes swept the shelves, lined with books and collections from her husband's travels. His desk was strewn with records of sale and shipping schedules. The library was unkempt and in need of fresh air, but at first glance, nothing seemed amiss.

She scanned the room again, looking for remnants of primal engagement—a discarded fan, an errant floral decoration, a forgotten handbag. But there was nothing. What was curious, however, was a collection of playing cards tacked to the backside of the door. She would not have noticed them had she not edged the door closed to conceal her movements from snooping servants.

The Jacks were aligned horizontally and represented each of the suits—hearts, diamonds, clubs, and spades. There were hash marks underneath, as if to keep score in a game. They were deep groves in the wood—scars not made on a whim and not possible to erase. Florie traced the fissures in the grain, wondering how inebriated her husband must have been to allow this defacement of his home. She also pondered his choice to tack the cards there, making the playing deck useless for contests. Something was not right about this scene, but she could not place her finger on what that was.

Florie backed away from the door, as if this perspective might reveal more secrets. She hoped the shifting light might offer the missing piece. Her gaze returned to the hashmarks, deep and uneven like scratches from a trapped animal. Or revenge from a wronged wife.

Turning her attention back to the rest of the room, she shook her head at the lack of care with which the men had left the place. Off to London they were, to conduct business and no doubt visit a brothel. Though she balked at this, Florie was no saint, for her time with Jim Maybrick had taught her to engage in private activities of her own. Each lurid letter she wrote, each clandestine tryst, they all were scores against him, even if he was unaware.

They were her hashmarks in the door of their marriage.

Just thinking about such things made her face warm—with desire, triumph, and a tinge of regret. The man she'd met upon the S.S. Baltic once upon a time was but a memory in the wind; after he had won her, his true colors were revealed. And Florie couldn't help but wonder if there were deeper shades still—more sinister ones. The monster had shown itself to her only once or twice, when he'd struck her in a fit of rage. Then it retreated into its hole inside him with recoiling shame.

As Florie moved back toward her husband's desk, she noticed the cover had been left off his inkwell—something he had surely done while intoxicated. A drawer was also slightly ajar, and it called to her. The journal that lay there looked no different than other ledgers that contained merchant information, yet inside was a hornet's nest on which Florie was about to step.

The cover was soft leather and lined inside with red cloth. The first page was marked with a wax seal normally used to close letters—it was strange ornament, for it did not seal anything that Florie could see. The red wax was emblazed with the initials R.S., which she could not place despite thinking of all their acquaintances.

As she turned the pages, they shifted in their stitching and revealed multiple entries written by various hands. But most of it sounded like nonsense. One read: She slept on the street as the sky rained down tears and washed away her dirt. Another read: She was a marvelous mare to break and her smile is etched evermore.

She recognized her husband's script, making out what looked like rules. One—our fellowship is closed to new members. Two—we will not speak of our activities outside of this room. Three—we will take our shared secrets to the grave. Four—if one falls before the others, he will take the blame.

And when she turned the page, Florie found four thumb prints as signatures, bold and brown-red, beneath the words:

The Ripper Society. *A gentleman's club?* She stared at the page with growing unease, for clearly the men were up to no good. But this document did not confess anything specific—just a bond of men entrenched in libertine ways. *Ripper.* Why would they choose that name? She thought of the headlines of Jack the Ripper, terrifying London, and she felt glad that she was far away in Liverpool. *Ripper.* It echoed in her mind, crept up the back of her neck.

And then she knew.

Her glance flew to the back of the door, where the eyes of the stoic Jacks watched. They mocked her in silence and tainted the very air she breathed. The hash marks burned in the door, taking on a whole new meaning. She could hear them sinking deeper into the oak, scratching and scraping, among a backdrop of women's screams that echoed from the streets of London—all the way to Liverpool.

Florie's hands shook as she replaced the journal back into the drawer, pushed it close quietly. Then she reviewed her movements, reminding herself she hadn't touched anything, hadn't moved a thing. She closed the door behind her, sliding the lock back into its place and then dropped the key on the floor as if her husband had lost it in haste. *He must never know… lest he do the same to me as what's been done to those women.* The very thought made her breath catch in her throat, her heart race, her skin creep with spiders.

It wasn't until she was halfway up the stairs to her room that she heard the carriage outside. The men were not quiet as they entered the home, complaining about the rain and their grumbling bellies. They were supposed to be en route to

London. Jim must have realized his key was missing. *Did he suspect it was me? Did he know?*

Florie lurked in the hallway upstairs, just out of their vision. But she could hear everything.

"Jim, you fool, you dropped it on our way out," said one of the male voices. She couldn't tell which man to whom it belonged. She imagined her husband bending to retrieve the key she had placed there on purpose.

Another said, "Now, let me grab my prizes, too." The library door creaked opened.

"I know the box was here." The voices were muffled now.

"Perhaps you left it in the carriage."

"Or dropped it on the way in."

They searched and grumbled, shifting papers and turning over chairs until they decided to give up the search.

"She was my first, you know," said one of the men as they made their way back out of doors.

"There are many other prizes to be had," said Jim. "It will be easy to replace."

It was then that Florie recalled the snuff box she'd pocketed when examining the library. She pulled it out of her pocket, hidden deep in the folds of her skirts, and examined the ornate silver box. Deep flourishes of flowers and vines decorated the top, and it rattled curiously as she turned it over.

When she opened it, there was not snuff but a collection of what looked like pebbles at first glance. Florie pinched one between her thumb and forefinger, examining the small object with a crater on one end.

They were human teeth, browned and worn and dead.

So startled was Florie that she dropped the trinket and its prized contents, spilling them all over the floor of her lavish home. And as she picked up the remnants of another woman's life, it was then that it came to her—she must murder her husband.

Florie's mind spun down a dark hole, following images of female bodies slashed and butchered. *What kind of demon could do such a thing?* Even at her worst, she could never cut a person intentionally; even the thought of butchering a chicken turned her stomach. *Leave it to wicked men to make a contest out of murder.* So disgusted was she that she almost wretched right there on her Persian rug.

Feelings of vengeance burned in her chest—for herself and the countless other women betrayed by this circle of darkness—this Ripper Society. For that society these days—ripping out the souls of women. The mothers, sisters, daughters, and brides. The teachers, nursemaids, and midwives. Even the barmaids and harlots. No one deserved this.

The resolution was simple and poetic: just as he had entrapped her, so should fly paper be his undoing. The plans unfolded quickly, like they were already there, waiting to be found. The arsenical compound was not hard to extract from the paper, and because he already willfully ingested the substance, all she had to do was tip the scales a bit further.

It would begin upon his return. She had preparations to make. And it would not be for one—but four. The stoic Jacks, with their cruel ways and brutal intentions, would burn from the inside out.

 This piece originally appeared in *Historic Tales: Collection of Short Stories*, Free Spirit, 2022.

She Has Seen the Wolf:
A Secret Thread from
The Butterfly Circle Trilogy

Cleveland, Ohio, U.S.A.

November, 1994.

The wolf's yellow eyes glowered at Kate Simoson from within
the painting. At first glance they were two golden disks against
darkness, hanging in the air like enchanted moons. But upon
closer inspection, murky fur obscured by trees emerged, with
flecks of gray and brown against black. The creature stalked
his prey in shadow, with silhouettes of branches reaching
toward a midnight sky. In the foreground stood a girl, cloaked
in red and holding a basket, her face hidden in the cowl of her
cape.

He was hunting her.

The painting once hung at her grandparents' house in the
guest bedroom Kate frequented as a child. She would wake in
the middle of the night to find the wolf's eyes upon her,
shifting in the moonlight. The image was at once a harbinger
of nightmares and a fairy tale that invited her in. As a five-year
old, the painting had unnerved her. She *was* the little girl in
red. But now, at twenty-five, she related to its darkness.

Kate stared back at it, mentally becoming the wolf as she sat at
her Nana's table, a warm oak circle in a bright yellow kitchen.
Stacks of papers and books stood like a barrier between her

and the painting. It hung on the opposite wall, watching as she toiled through her master's thesis, analyzing versions of "Little Red Riding Hood" in literature and pop culture. Thoughts on Perrault, the Brothers Grimm, and a smattering of writers from other cultures and times swam in her mind.

Her eyes fell onto the blank page, longing for elusive inspiration. She had hoped that returning to her hometown over the Thanksgiving holiday might stir some passion or insight, or at the very least, help her fill pages.

> "Into the woods, and through the trees
> To where I am expected ma'am
> Into the woods to grandmother's house
> Are you certain of your way?"
>
> ~ Sondheim, *Into the Woods*, The Musical

She stared at Little Red's lyrics, considering their irony, then turned her gaze out the window, past the line of porcelain sparrows, where she looked for answers among storm clouds. The sun hid behind gray billowing masses, holding her in shadow. The Cleveland sky was a metaphor for her life at present—ominous and unclear.

A wave of nausea crept up from her stomach and she swallowed, cursing the thing she'd been trying to forget all morning. But the image burned in her mind no matter what she did to erase it.

Positive. The test had been positive.

"Coffee?" asked Nana as she joined Kate in the kitchen. She'd never been one of those grandmothers who made tea. It was always Café Du Monde, all the way from New Orleans. She'd never been, but Nana was in love with the French Quarter and all its secrets. She always returned from her trips with little bits of myth and lore, weaving in sightings of Voo Doo priestesses and ghosts of long-dead writers. Nana had always been eccentric, and it was one of the things Kate loved best about her.

"Thank you," said Kate, watching the steam rise from the artsy, one-of-a-kind mug from Nana's collection.

"I hope your Mom is able to enjoy some Thanksgiving dinner this week," Nana said, a question more than a statement. Her lapis blue earrings dangled in large drops, swinging back and forth from her lobes.

Kate nodded, sipping the warmth and breathing deeply as the coffee melted into her body. "She'll be working at the ER all Thanksgiving night, but Dad will have dinner for her on Friday. You know how she is—doesn't mind doing holidays early or late as long as it doesn't mess with her work schedule."

Nana smiled, the pride clear on her face. "My girl, saving lives."

Kate felt a tinge of guilt. Her mother, far away in her Southern Ohio home, had hoped she would follow in her footsteps in healthcare. But that gene had skipped Kate's generation, along with other things her Mom had hoped for, like predictability and a stable career path.

"Well," said Kate. "I only wish I had the stomach for blood, then I might have maintained the legacy."

Nana shook her head. "You've got to follow your heart, honey. See where all this research takes you." She swished her hand in the air like a spell. "Maybe teaching, maybe writing. Lots of noble professions out there."

"Tell that to Mom," said Kate.

Nana paused, taking a sip from her mug. "Nursing wasn't my first choice, you know."

Kate looked up, meeting Nana's eyes. It was the first she'd ever heard this. "Really?" she said. "The way Mom talks about you, it's like you always knew, always had a plan."

Nana raised her eyebrows. "No. Not always," she said. "I wanted to be a writer. But things happen—they change you." She sighed, far away for a minute. "Well, I'm glad you're here—even if it's just for the week."

Nana pushed a plate of muffins a bit closer to Kate. They were normally her favorite—blueberry with a sprinkle of sugar on top—but today they evoked waves of nausea she struggled to swallow.

"Eat, honey, you look so thin," Nana said, not realizing the effect they might have. Kate wasn't sure if it was the proximity or that sweet smell, but her stomach protested promptly.

"Oh," she said, not thinking clearly to form a more cohesive sentence. She jumped up, putting distance between herself and the muffins and ran as quickly as she could toward the bathroom, leaving Nana staring after her.

*

That afternoon, tired from her early morning flight and frustrated with writer's block, Kate headed to the guest bedroom for a nap. She took the old stairs slowly, listening to the familiar creak beneath her weight, wondering if Nana had figured out her secret. When she'd come back to the table after retching in the bathroom, there was a look of knowing in her eyes. Kate had avoided them with her own, a matching shade of cornflower that always revealed too much. And just like Nana, she often saw things that others didn't—hints of body language, symbolism hidden in artwork, layered meaning in old literature for which most had no patience. But it always led her back to the darkness, like an elusive secret she couldn't quite catch.

Kate stared at the back of the closed door, wondering if she should just get it out in the open. Go downstairs and confess what she was holding inside. Part of her wished Nana had already figured it out. But what would she say? Would she pressure her to keep the baby? Would she tell her parents? No, it was best to keep it to herself, within her own realm of influence.

Kate opened the cover of the book she'd found on Nana's coffee table, eager to distract herself with what might be a relevant source for her thesis. *Legend of the Rougarou: The Swamp Werewolf.* It was a stretch, but she wondered if there could be a "Little Red Riding Hood" connection.

The cover was a fantastic painting of a southern swamp with trees that spread out at the base then dove under the water. Debris drifted on the surface, leaves, algae, nests of bugs. And who knew what lurked beneath the curtain. Alligators, snakes, and maybe even…

Kate turned the hard-back cover, and the spine cracked. It had been a long time since she'd heard such a sound; it brought a rush of distant childhood memories of afternoons spent on the couch cuddled up against Nana, reading storybooks until they fell asleep. On the inside was an inscription: *With love, from your sister.* An insignia of a rose was beneath the words, sketched delicately in pencil.

Sister. Nana had no sister. Maybe it was bought from a used bookstore. Those were the best kind anyway—their aged pages holding the essence of all who had skimmed them before.

Each was a bound haunted house.

She turned the page, and the face of the werewolf lunged out at her. The illustration was detailed, with each hair a slice on paper. The eyes were at once ferocious and captivating, even in their gray tones. The claws, fingers with needle points atop them, reached out from the book, ready to shred prey in long strokes.

It was deliciously haunting.

The next page was where the text began, pulling her into the southeast United States, through swamps and into rural countryside, in between myths and legends, where she imagined the bones of slaves and slaveholders now rested. If there was any place that might be haunted, it would be there. Land could hold the memory of those who'd walked it. How she longed to visit such places, to feel beneath the layers of reality to what lurked on the other side.

Her eyes slipped along the pages in a gentle rhythm, taking in the words and imagining the deep, dark forest. The places that lay just beyond a person's awareness, in Freud's uncanny valley. She ran with the Rougarou through the swamp, its breath hot in her ears, its wild, insatiable appetite twisting her stomach. She lulled between sleeping and waking, where dreams reach out to grab hold of your insides.

It was when she had started to doze off that the book wavered and a picture fell out from between the pages. She was startled awake. Even upside down, she recognized the image. It was a black and white photo taken lying down—an image of the sky with shadowed branches reaching out from the sides. Dramatic and poetic, just as they had been—she and her best friend Bea.

"We always have the sky," Kate whispered, still drowsy, touching it at the corner, careful not to soak in too much of its magic. It was something Nana had always said—a mantra they had adopted and shared.

Tenderness came first, followed by a slew of poison—anger, resentment, bitterness. Kate gulped the spiked emotion down. Her brow furrowed in frustration. Kate sat up. Why did Nana have this here, tucked into a book like a sharp knife waiting to cut the unsuspecting?

The picture held her hostage.

It had been taken on the Fourth of July when Bea's mother was working at the hospital with her own mom, and Nana was hosting dinner. Of course, Bea was invited—she was always invited—for wherever Kate went, Bea was not far behind. This had been her friend's gift to Nana, the photo at the center of the collage that had won her the Ohio Arts Prize their sophomore year. She'd taken it lying down beside Kate in Nana's backyard, invoking her grandmother's saying that meant no matter where you go, you just look up and we are connected—all of us in the family.

And that included Bea.

Kate had made sure it did.

Until it didn't. Until she broke their hearts, stole from Nana's purse, lied and cheated and became a creature no one recognized. Kate let out a long, drawn-out breath, exhaling the worry and the pain and the broken memories that Bea took with her when she entered that other life—the one that stole her from them all.

Kate had moved away and never looked back. Not once. Well, at least after that last letter she sent, saying goodbye to Bea forever.

She tucked the photo back into the book and set it on the bedside table, hoping the Rougarou inside would eat it and wipe away her memories for good. They were no more than ghosts.

*

That evening, Kate and Nana sat like bookends on the couch, the warmth of the fire a respite. Kate pulled the quilt over her legs, still feeling woozy from the meal that she was able to eat and even enjoy without nausea. The first snow of the season fell outside, the flakes like confetti under the streetlights.

Nana held a glass of merlot, the color a deep scarlet in the firelight. Kate had passed on the offer for a glass, despite her longing for the rich, velvety liquid. Nana had looked at her directly, as if she expected the response.

She knows, thought Kate.

But Nana didn't ask, and Kate didn't confess. The photo was still on her mind, but Kate held that in as well, hoping it would fade into the recesses of her mind. She waited for Nana to turn on the TV, distract them both for the night, but instead, she pulled a large book from the coffee table and placed it between them.

"Go on," Nana said. "Take a look."

Kate picked up the oversized hardcover. There was a drawn symbol on the front, four circles intertwined, tucked in between ribbon and lace.

She opened the scrapbook to the first page, where an image of a mansion was pasted. Beneath it read *Prescott House*. Two pages in, Kate looked up at Nana.

"An unwed mothers' home?" she asked.

The bohemian Nana she knew, so full of love and joy, was the most distant thing from the forlorn girl who had written in the scrapbook.

Nana nodded, but she said nothing. It was her way—*being* rather than speaking when the topic was difficult. Often it was the silence between them that felt like shelter. It was something Kate's mother couldn't stand, swore up and down that her parents' generation was all about sweeping dirty secrets under the rug. It was why her mother was so direct—too direct at times. Kate preferred a happy medium, a balance between privacy and sharing. She saw this as an invitation—to meet her Nana half-way.

"So mom…" Kate started the thought, hoping Nana would finish it.

"No," said Nana. "She wasn't the baby."

The silence hung between them as a line Kate didn't want to cross. Her mother had no siblings, so Nana must have given the baby up for adoption. The words were out of her mouth before she could rein them in.

"What happened to the baby?" She had too much of her mother in her.

Nana's lips parted but nothing emerged. She took a sip of wine—the last sip, then leaned forward.

"I lost it," she said. "But not until the end."

"Oh," said Kate. "I'm sorry."

Nana shrugged. "It was the way it was meant to be. What I did get out of it, though, were lifelong friends." She smiled, recalling another time. "I thought you might like to read it. Look through the pictures." She tilted her head in suggestion. "Maybe it will help you in some way."

It was Kate's turn to invite the silence. She wasn't ready to confirm her circumstances. Not yet.

Nana stood. "Don't stay up too late, honey." Then she walked toward the kitchen, paused in the doorway. "Catch," she said, tossing a kiss toward her granddaughter.

Kate smiled and reached out her hand to catch the air kiss, then turned the page of the scrapbook to disappear into Nana's keepsake.

*

Kate woke early the next morning still on Nana's couch, the scrapbook open and balanced on the arm cushion, waiting for her attention. Though she'd been in Cleveland since yesterday, it took her a moment to remember where she was. She lingered there, half awake, sinking back into her body and becoming aware of the small, warm figure cuddled up to her stomach. Wink, Nana's rich grey tabby, had curled up into a ball and nestled into Kate, purring gently.

Her problems came back to her then, one after the other, a stone at a time. The pregnancy. The thesis. Her dwindling bank account. What seemed like a fork in the road loomed before her, two paths that diverged. Kate recalled Delarue's musings in the French tradition of Little Red, where the wolf offered two paths to the girl—a choice between pins and needles. Both were sharp, both cut, but one might be used to mend while the other was a temporary fix, meant for something impermanent.

What is it, Kate? She thought. *Pins or needles?*

And suddenly the thought was too much. Just last week, motherhood had been a distant possibility, not so much as peeking over the horizon. And yet now here it was, a looming threat that had taken up residence inside her.

Kate's lungs felt heavy as she took a deep breath. Wink shifted against her, reached out her legs to stretch, and she couldn't help but imagine the cat was an infant, lulling her into the future. Or she might be a little wolf, ready to devour her from the inside out. Yes, that felt more apropos, especially considering the father—that cheating son of a bitch. His face flashed in her mind—his very handsome face. He was her very own Newland Archer.

Kate bit her lip and huffed as she shifted on the couch, wondering if Edith Wharton had written from her own experience or breathed life into the characters strictly from imagination. Kate breathed through a wave of nausea and shoved her thoughts into the back of her mind. Her neck protested as she pulled her head upright, and Wink glared at her in annoyance. She had been quite content in the curl of Kate's body.

The floor creaked under Kate's feet as she stood—old wooden boards that had been part of the fabric of her childhood. Her melancholy was interrupted by a rush from the past, a memory of her grandfather playing his guitar by the fireplace. A smile appeared upon her lips almost by surprise. Her gaze fell upon the instrument, which stood silent now, keeping vigil over the house.

Her grandfather's presence was everywhere, though he'd been gone for almost ten years. Kate approached the silent guitar, afraid to disturb its peace. Her grandfather had passed so suddenly, so young. Kate pushed the memories of that day away, tried to refocus on his laughter, his music. She had only been fifteen at the time, still a girl with impossible hopes and far-away dreams. In many ways his death also marked the loss of that innocence.

Kate's eyes returned to the scrapbook on the couch, where it lay open, inviting her back into the past, to a place where unwed motherhood was the equivalent of shame. She thought of Nana as the young woman who'd written those words, so alone and without hope and eerily similar to how Kate was feeling now. Was single motherhood much more accepted in the 1990s? It didn't feel that way, even if unwed mothers' homes were a thing of the past.

"She has seen the wolf." These words hung over Kate's head, swimming in and out of her ears, not letting her forget her own predicament. In her research, she had discovered this was a saying long ago to describe a girl who was no longer a virgin—a French connection if she remembered right. It was yet another way to shame women for their own sexuality. It made her think of chastity belts and the like. Surely the saying had been developed by a man—or a bitter, repressed woman.

Kate ran her fingers over the scrapbook's mint green cover, its edges aged and soft. The lace and ribbons that had been pasted there were delicate and yellowed with time. The four joined circles were crudely drawn, uneven in their overlap, which made them more endearing. She picked the book up, flipped through its pages gingerly, careful not to let anything fall out. A lock of red hair—braided. A necklace with a heart locket—empty. Train ticket stubs—mostly from Ohio with a destination of Louisiana but with many stops in between. Postcards from all over—other parts of Ohio, New York, California, Massachusetts—all signed with a drawn rose. It was the same as the one from the inscription in the book she found the other night about the Rougarou.

There were black and white photos, too. One of a young woman with dark eyes and hair, whose sensuality was like that of a movie star. Another of two women—one with large light eyes and another with freckles sprinkled across her nose. They held each other in an embrace. And then there was the one she was drawn to the most—a pale-eyed beauty with light hair, with a look of innocence that had been chased away too soon.

Nana.

Kate touched the edges of the photo, enchanted by the image. She plucked it gently from its holders, untucking the corners carefully so as not to damage it. The other side indicated only "1950." Two years after she was sent to the home. She must have been about 18.

Kate tried to connect the girl to the woman she knew as her Nana. She was more layered and complicated than she had imagined. Maybe her grandfather had not been Nana's first love. Maybe he had not been Nana's first sexual encounter. There was something utterly beautiful about seeing Nana through a wider lens.

She wanted to know more.

*

It was mid-morning before Kate had an appetite, but she quickly realized the bagel was a mistake. When Kate had purged the evil in her belly, she wrapped herself in a blanket, pulled the spare pair of boots by the door onto her feet, and ventured into the backyard.

She breathed the crisp air in, the smell of fallen leaves filling her with memories of hayrides, bonfires, and trips to Patterson's Apple Farm. She walked to grandfather's green chair and sat, pulling a book out from the folds of the blanket. The cover of Angela Carter's *The Bloody Chamber* mimicked pencil with cross-hatching. The wolf held a door knocker in its mouth against a background of filigree. On the back was a fleur de lis, and it made Kate pause, considering any potential connection the English writer might have had with France, New Orleans, or any religious connotation. It was something she would have to research.

Kate turned to the tale she had read many times, "The Company of Wolves," and considered the film adaptation that Carter herself cowrote. In the film, a girl is trapped in a dream, stalked by a werewolf who is both dashing and dangerous, and despite warnings from her grandmother, she longs for a kiss from this seductive creature. The story in her collection is much shorter, and this is where Kate's interest lies. It was the language, the description and metaphor that drew her in where "the forest closed upon her like a pair of jaws" (Carter 146). Kate read and reread the line, imagining not only the scene but the feelings it evoked.

Gnashing teeth coming down upon her like a prison cell.

Locking her in with no way out.

Trapping her forever down one path into that deep, dark, place called motherhood.

"Morning, honey." Nana's voice jarred Kate out of her thoughts and startled the birds that had gathered around the feeders.

"Morning," Kate said, shaking off the lingering metaphorical vice that had been tightening around her.

"What are you doing out here?" Nana asked.

Kate held up the book. "Just needed some fresh air."

Nana nodded, pulled her sweater more tightly around her shoulders.

"Coffee and talk?"

"Sure," said Kate, looking up into the skeletal trees one last time.

"When you're ready," said Nana, then disappeared back into the house, leaving the door slightly ajar.

*

Kate and Nana sat at the oak table, Wink on a third chair like she had been invited to the conversation. The hot liquid steamed between them, rising up from inside of the cup like an apparition.

Nana swept a silver lock of hair from her forehead. "So, you've been reading?"

Kate breathed in the aroma of coffee and chicory, took a sip. She motioned to the book on the table.

"Well, this is for my thesis," she said, "But I've also read your scrapbook. Not all of it yet." She paused, not sure how to bridge the unspoken. "Knowing you went through all that. Why didn't you ever tell me?"

Nana took a breath, exhaled in a long, lingering hush. "Well, I told your mother when she was a teenager. And that didn't go over so well."

Kate thought of her mom, a proponent of openness and honesty at all cost.

"That's hard to imagine," Kate said.

"I think she felt lied to," said Nana. "Frustrated that I hadn't told her sooner. But it wasn't something I thought would be helpful—to her or me—when she was young. I didn't want her to see my relationship with your grandfather differently."

Kate nodded. "That makes sense."

"I was worried she would think of it as less if she knew he wasn't the first man in my life," said Nana. "But the truth is, he was more special *because* of the bad experiences I'd had prior to meeting him. He was my knight in shining armor in so many ways."

"He definitely had 'knight on the horse' vibes," said Kate, smiling fondly.

"But he wasn't perfect. I wasn't perfect. We were imperfect together. And it worked. But not because it was always easy or because we'd had some fairy tale life before we met," said Nana. "We knew what it was like to *not* be loved well."

They fell into silence, sipping coffee and watching the sunlight play through the branches outside.

"And what about the dreams," said Kate. "You reference *the wolf* all throughout the scrapbook." She gestured to the pile of papers that sat on the counter like a ghost. "I mean…"

"Yes," began Nana. "I… have some explaining to do."

Kate raised her eyebrows, waited.

"When you started having dreams as a child, talking about a wolf. Well, I thought it was a coincidence. I hoped it was, anyway," said Nana. "It was my fault because I had that painting in the guest bedroom where you slept when you stayed the night." She waved at the wolf painting on the wall. "So, I moved it. Hoped it would stop."

"It didn't," Kate said.

"I know," said Nana. "I mean, I didn't know at the time. I realized it later, when your mom told me you were still having nightmares."

Silence hung in the air for a moment. They both found themselves staring at the painting, drawn into the eyes that watched them back.

"I don't want secrets to linger anymore," said Nana, "I have a feeling you're ready to know these things about me. Something tells me you can relate."

Her eyes drifted to Kate's midsection, hidden beneath the lip of the table.

The breath caught in Kate's throat. She gulped. "When did you know?" she asked. "About me?"

"The nausea was a clue," said Nana. "I thought, either the flu or..."

Kate nodded, sipped her coffee.

"Do you love him?" asked Nana.

Kate couldn't stop the sarcastic laugh from escaping.

"No. Definitely not. He was... a mistake." She paused, gulped. "I hope you don't think less of me," Kate continued.

"Oh, honey," said Nana. "No. Listen, a woman's journey is complex. And private. I love you—that'll never change. And I'll never think any less of you for making mistakes. God knows I've made plenty."

Kate licked her lips. "So, is what you wrote true? I mean, I understand the unwed mothers' home. But the hole in the wall, the dreams. The seances. The... ghost wolf," she swished her hand in the air, searching for the words. "Was it escapism? Imagination? You said you wanted to be a writer."

Nana's lips turned up a little at the corners. She leaned forward, reached into the front of her shirt and pulled out something that hung from a chain there. And what emerged was a key—one with four adjoining circles at the top.

"What do *you* think?" she said.

It wasn't the first time Kate had wanted to believe in the power of other realms—magic, the supernatural. But it was unusual for anyone outside of her own head to corroborate it—even her Nana, with her love of culture and art. She was accustomed to hiding those dalliances deep in her internal world. She knew she would just be seen as childish, chasing the whims of fantasy.

"What are you saying?" said Kate. "Those things you wrote about in the scrapbook—the visions, the ghosts, the... *wolf*. They were real?"

Nana held her gaze.

"The most important part is the relationships—the friends," she said. "There are rare times in your life that someone opens their whole heart to you, inviting you into their world, their pain. You're connected from that point, for good or bad. That type of bond can't be broken—damaged, yes, tarnished, certainly—but never broken, despite years and miles and growing up and growing old. And that's the most real thing I learned there."

"But, yes. The other things were real, too. As real as they could have been for a group of teenage girls imprisoned in an old mansion—and their bodies, if I'm being honest. Sometimes we try to take the magic out of life, thinking it'll help us see more clearly—to focus on realistic problems. Like your mom. That's her way. But maybe the magic has been there all along. We just forget how to see it if we stop looking for too long. I don't ever want to stop seeing it."

Nana's lips turned up slightly at the corners.

"You're not gonna give me a clear answer, are you?" asked Kate. "Like, evidence."

"Evidence of magic?" Nana laughed gently. "I think you know as well as I do that we have to see something first-hand to know for sure," said Nana, standing to rinse out her coffee cup. She turned on the faucet, filled it with water, dumped it out. Then she turned back to Kate. "Maybe the wolf isn't *your* ghost. But that doesn't mean you can't learn something from it. Hauntings can be older than you—much older. I hope my story helps. Maybe it will lead you in a new direction. Give you some more things to research."

*

As she stepped off the public bus, Kate tucked her scarf around her neck and walked briskly against the stinging wind onto the Cleveland State University campus. Lake Erie was several miles away, but its fury whipped the air even this far offshore; Kate had forgotten just how fierce the lake wind could be.

Her face felt battered by the time she made it through the door of the library, where she entered the elevator deep in the bowels of Rhodes Tower. She was hopeful this trip would not be for nothing, but earlier that day Nana claimed their reference collection had a lot to offer. In fact, she was so insistent that Kate go, she had started to wonder if her presence was too much for Nana. Maybe she was already wearing out her welcome.

The library was open two days before Thanksgiving, no doubt for students who were completing final papers for the looming end-of-semester deadline. It was busier than she'd expected, too, with clusters of students huddled around tables and others searching through stacks for just the right resource. The fourth floor was quiet, with few hovering bodies browsing and several tucked into corners. The air smelled of old books and Pine-Sol.

After a quick peek in the card catalog, Kate had her destination—the literature section that held criticism and history of fairy tales. She had exhausted the research in the Ohio University library and was hoping to find some new sources here. But most of the volumes looked familiar, with the exception of one or two. She had more luck in the academic journals section, though, selecting multiple issues with relevant studies. "Red Riding Hood: An Interpretation from Anthropology" and "Jung's Archetypes in the Fairy Tale" looked particularly promising. They were less than she had hoped for, but at least she could add something.

She was on her way to the copy machine, prepared with a pocketful of coins and short pile of journals, when she was caught by surprise.

"Katie? Katie Simoson?" The female voice was barely more than a whisper for that was the only thing appropriate in the middle of a hushed library.

Kate turned to find a familiar, if older, face. The warm green eyes were brighter than the last time she had seen them. In her memory, they were sad and worn, rimmed with red and angry in the wake of lost dreams.

"Bea," Kate said, almost dropping the collection she had in her arms. The smile was on her face before she knew it, taking in a healthier version of her old friend. She was so surprised that her anger and resentment were absent.

In the next moment, Bea's arms were around her, squeezing her tightly. Soft, dirty blonde curls kissed her face. The scent of apple shampoo brought back a flood of memories. High school football games, walks in the park, dancing at weekend parties, and sharing late-night secrets while tucked into sleeping bags. And then the other, unwanted memories began to bubble to the surface—unreturned phone calls, a new crowd that ran too fast for Kate, getting the message that Bea had been sent to rehab.

When they parted, Bea took a long breath. "I can't believe it. Are you back? Are you going to school here?"

"Just visiting," said Kate, shoving the awkward feeling into the pit of her stomach. "At Nana's for Thanksgiving."

"Aw, Nana," said Bea, for she had been a permanent fixture in the afternoons and Nana and Grandfather's, too. "How is she? She still talks to my mom, but I haven't seen her since..." Her voice trailed off, a cloud falling on her light. Bea swallowed hard.

Kate knew what she didn't want to say. The funeral. It was Grandfather's funeral, and she had been high.

"She's good." Kate cut off the silence before it stretched too far between them.

"Look at us, trying to make small talk," said Bea, her face reddening the slightest bit.

"You look good," said Kate. "Happy."

Bea nodded. "Yeah," she said. "Sober for five years now." She gulped. "Look, I know I said a lot of this in the letters I sent, but..."

The letters Kate hadn't opened. *Couldn't* open.

"I'm really sorry," continued Bea. "For everything. I wasn't myself... for a long time. I hope you know that."

"I do," said Kate.

"And I know I can't take anything back. So, there's that." The tears began to well in Bea's eyes before she rolled them, blinked quickly. "Thank you for the letter you sent to me. For what you said."

I forgive you, but it will be a process. I don't know if I can ever trust you again. It's probably a good thing I'm moving. I do want you to heal and wish you well. Sincerely, Kate.

Sincerely. Not 'love', not 'best', not 'always', like a real friend might do. Just 'sincerely.' It was all she could give at the time.

"I understand," said Bea. "I do. I've had a lot of time to think over these years. About what I lost—*who* I lost."

"It's been a long time," said Kate.

"Um… Do you… would you want to grab a coffee?" Bea took a breath, exhaled. Waited.

If Kate had more time to consider she would have said no, would have kept the wall up. But it had already come crumbling down; something about being there with her in the same room changed things.

"Yeah," said Kate. "Yeah, okay."

"You free now?" Bea said, looking at her watch. "Or, rather, in about fifteen minutes? I'm almost off."

"Oh, you work here?" asked Kate, noticing the badge on her shirt for the first time.

"Grad Assistant," said Bea. "History. But also Library Aide for 20 hours a week." She shrugged. "It pays my tuition, though."

"Yeah, I get it. Me, too. English Lit," said Kate. "I do my GA time as a Writing Tutor at OU."

"Right—Ohio University. Not surprised about the English Lit," said Bea. "You always did like the stories. You still write?"

Kate nodded, the awkwardness creeping back in. "When I can," she said. She hoped this coffee was not a mistake.

"Hey, um, weird question," said Kate. "Do you know how to find out where an unwed mothers' home from the 1940s would be? Down on Euclid Avenue. Any idea?"

Bea's mouth opened, and her head tilted. "Um, I can try to pull that info for you. We've got all sorts of stuff on Cleveland history. Why?"

"Long story," said Kate. She hadn't thought about it long enough to be more careful.

Bea shrugged. "Yeah, okay. I'll go see what I can find. You copying?"

Kate nodded.

"I'll meet you in the copy room in just a few." With that, Bea disappeared down the aisle with a bounce in her step that Kate remembered but hadn't seen in quite some time. She was caught between surprise and caution, between hope and memory that was far too painful to conjure completely.

And it was too late to back out now.

*

While Bea maneuvered her Jeep Cherokee out of the Cleveland State parking garage and onto Chester Avenue, Kate sat in the passenger seat examining the photocopied pictures of historical unwed mothers' homes along with statistics and a general background in type. The images were black and white, mostly of female staff dressed in conservative uniforms and looking sullen. But there were also photographs of building façades, from hospital-style structures to old Victorian mansions.

"There are so many," said Kate. "I never would have thought that."

"So, why are you researching this?" asked Bea, her eyes on the road. Gray clouds had blocked out the sun, and a torrent of snow was quickly turning into a white-out. As they approached a red light, she slowed down, pumping her brakes to make sure they didn't slide into the intersection.

Kate breathed in deeply. "I just... had an idea for a story," she said, swallowing the secret.

"Oh," said Bea. "Well, that's great that you're still writing. I mean, no one could beat your ghost stories at camp, that's for sure. But you know, for someone who could tell them, you sure couldn't handle them from anywhere else."

Kate sniffed. "What is that supposed to mean?"

"Oh, come on," said Bea. "I have a long memory, KK."

Kate's heart softened at the use of her childhood nickname. KK for Kate Kendall—the first name was for her dad's mother, the middle one for Nana. "And?" said Kate.

"Seventh grade. Sarah Ford's basement. '*Silver Bullet*' with Corey Haim. I swear I never thought you'd sleep through the night again," said Bea.

Kate rolled her eyes at the memory. "It was that damn werewolf," she said.

"Yeah, I know," said Bea. "You kept the light on during every sleepover for the next three months."

Kate paused as she flipped through the papers, her eyes falling on one that looked familiar. The mansion was partly done in Tudor style and the rest in stone.

"This one," said Kate. "Prescott House. 745 Euclid Avenue." She glanced over at Bea in the driver's seat, whose eyes were glued to the road in front of them. "Can we drive by?" Kate asked.

"Now?" said Bea, looking over to measure how serious she was. "Um, I mean, I can drive up Euclid instead of Chester, but who knows where that address is exactly."

But she drove, and Kate looked, thinking about how oddly familiar it was to be sitting in the car with this friend who she had not seen in many years. And though time had separated them, and anger, and tears, and lots of things, somehow, she still felt like home.

*

It was twenty minutes before they came upon the property marked 745 Euclid, a few miles east of University Circle and Case Western Reserve University, where the buildings were boarded up and covered in graffiti. Kate stared out the window at the looming brick wall that stood between them and the old building. Atop it was a metal grating that threatened to poke prying hands, should they dare to climb and seek entry. And beyond she could see two castle-like towers, reaching up into the sky among the naked trees.

Bea had slowed the car to a crawl, easing them along the uneven sidewalk, now covered in snow. The white hid any trash that might be there, painting it in a pristine veil that begged for footprints. When they reached the gate, a wrought iron filigree masterpiece that stretched up into an arch, the car came to a stop.

"Well, there it is," said Bea. The tension was clear in her voice, and Kate felt a pang of guilt for dragging her this far down Euclid. As they had approached, she noticed people cloaked in hoods, lurking in doorways of abandoned businesses, probably up to no good. But the lure of the unwed mothers' home pulled her with invisible tethers.

"Two minutes," said Kate, "I promise." She opened the door and stepped out into the cool air that swirled around her in a mix of snow and chill. The wind that had been so fierce further downtown but did not dare disturb this place.

"I don't think—" began Bea, but Kate had already slammed the door.

Kate marked the velvet white blanket with her steps, moving closer to peek through the lace of iron. She stared through the black metal curls to the building beyond, a dark body with a snow-covered roof and shuttered eyes. There was no sign of life—not a breath or a heartbeat.

The hush was both haunting and inviting.

Kate's eyes traveled along its lines—harsh towers that declared power and soft curves of aging eaves. She thought of Nana coming to this place as a girl, pregnant and afraid. She thought of Nana's friends, the ones she wrote about so fondly, and imagined them up in one of the rooms, laughing and crying and holding onto each other for dear life, not knowing what lay in store for their futures. She wanted to touch it—that past—walk in its memory, up the stairs to the hole in the wall, through the tunnels, and into the heart of Prescott House's legacy.

As Kate reimagined Nana's past, her breath rose in the air, a smoky trail of wishes and hopes. If she was among them, would her burden be easier to carry? At least it would be less lonely. Her hand rose to her womb, rested there on the cold fabric of her Nana's borrowed winter coat.

How had it come to this, that she was also an unwed mother?

"It's getting dark," said Bea, breaking the spell. She joined her friend and stood in silence for a moment. "Wow, look at these rosettes," she said, reaching out to touch the gate. "So Victorian."

Kate said nothing, barely aware of anything but the house and her own body.

"Katie." Bea's voice was softer now. "I really shouldn't be here… this close to temptation."

Kate tore her gaze away from the home, realizing for the first time that Bea wasn't nervous about the bad neighborhood. It was more than that.

Their eyes met and something passed between them.

"This isn't just about a story, is it?" said Bea, glancing down at Kate's hand on her abdomen.

*

The Arabica Coffee House on Coventry buzzed with laughter and the sound of steaming milk. The air was filled with notes of cinnamon and honey and wrapped around Kate as she and Bea wove their way to an empty table, holding their drinks—a nonfat decaf mocha for Kate and a chai latte for Bea.

As Kate took a seat, she felt the ghost of her younger self hovering somewhere, wearing too much lipstick and a low-cut top that left little to the imagination. She sighed, longing for the days when things were all about secrets and who was going to ask her to the homecoming dance.

Her eyes rose to meet Bea's, staring back at her, thoughtfully.

"What?" asked Kate.

Bea shrugged, chose her words carefully. "I know there's something going on with you. I can feel it. I'm not saying you have to tell me what it is, but I'm working on this radical honesty thing. So, I'm just putting it out there."

As much as she wanted to, Kate didn't look away.

"I'm pregnant," she said.

Bea nodded, not surprised. "I had a feeling. Your hands were lingering on your stomach while you stood out there, in front of that house." She sipped her latte, wiped the foam off her lip. "Is that a good thing?"

"No," said Kate. As soon as the word was out of her mouth, she felt guilty. "I mean… I want to be a mom someday, but not like this. Not in grad school making barely enough to cover my rent, with a guy I really don't like—and definitely don't love." The confession was like a pressure release. The words tumbled out, followed by a rush of emotions and tears that refused to stay locked up.

Bea sat and listened. She didn't argue, which is what her younger self would have done. She didn't cut Kate off, even though Kate wished she would. She didn't try to convince Kate what the right decision was or tell her how she should feel. She just listened.

It was ten minutes or so before Kate felt purged of her secret. Her shoulders had finally dropped. "My parents don't know," Kate said. "Just you and Nana."

"And the father?" asked Bea. "Does he know?"

Kate shook her head.

"Do you know what you want to do?"

Kate shook her head again.

Bea nodded. The lack of judgement was a relief, but sharing made Kate feel raw on the inside. She searched for a way to shift gears.

"That place today," began Kate. "I kind of want to go back. Check out the inside."

Bea's eyebrows rose. "Why do I feel like we're in fifth grade and you're convincing me to follow you down into the ravine by Roxboro to explore the Shaker steps in the dark?"

The memory of their misadventures came rushing back to Kate. Bea had come out of that with a broken arm, trying to rescue a baby bird who had fallen into the creek.

"Or," said Bea, not giving Kate a minute to jump in. "That time you wanted to see what the old boarded up church looked like down on 55th. Got a nasty cut on my ankle that day—you're lucky I didn't get tetanus."

Kate smirked. "I remember you did get a photo that won you honorable mention in some contest though," she said.

Bea rolled her eyes and shrugged. "Yeah, yeah. I'm just saying. You have a way of getting us into trouble." She paused, remembering the gap in time—the gap in their relationship. "Had a way, anyway."

The admission rained on them, pulling them back into the present.

"We had some good times," said Kate.

Bea nodded. "The best." She took another sip of latte. It used to be cigarettes that filled the silence with smoke when she didn't know what to say. Now it was just steam.

Kate was on the edge, looking over, wondering if she should step off the cliff. She licked her lips, remembered the broken piles of wood Bea had climbed on top of to get that shot in the church, when the setting sun peered through the stain glass window at just the right angle. As soon as she'd clicked the shutter on the camera, she'd come tumbling down.

Her life had been empty without Bea in it. She'd had friends since, sure. But none she would let in like Bea had been—her soul sister, her confidante. It was as if she'd been walking around without an arm for the last five years. And here she was, as familiar as she had always been, if a little worn.

Kate tapped the side of her cup, watching the steam rise. "I do want to go back," she said. "But I don't want to go alone." She looked at Bea, trying to measure her reaction. "If we just went once—during the day, when you're in the right head space... would you go?"

Bea offered a half-smile—the one that only shows up when she's nervous. It was her tell. "I don't know, KK."

"What if I told you it might be part of the Underground Railroad?" asked Kate. It was her trump card.

The humor left Bea's eyes and she leaned forward. "I'm listening."

*

They sat in Nana's driveway in the warmth of Bea's Jeep, heat blowing and the radio turned down to a hum. The sky had darkened and large snowflakes drifted down from the heavens, floating in the streetlights like fairy dust.

"You want to come in?" asked Kate, still caught off guard by how easily they had fallen back into a comfortable pattern. Time and pain may have separated them, but so much had remained the same. Bea's laugh and her jokes that skimmed too close to inappropriate had not changed at all.

"Nah, I should head to a meeting," she said.

"Hey, I'm sorry about taking you to that neighborhood without warning you," said Kate. "I didn't realize it would put you…"

"Don't apologize for my past," said Bea. "It's my problem, not yours. And, hey, we'll go back tomorrow in the daylight, and I'll be in the right head-space for a ravine adventure." She shrugged. "Maybe I'll get another great pic."

"No broken arms this time," said Kate.

"Or cut ankles," said Bea. She paused, faltered over her words. "Thank you for today. I really missed you, KK."

Kate nodded. "Me, too," she said, knowing how true that was, though she hadn't even been aware of it before today. Her eyes went to the window, where she thought she saw Nana's silhouette peering out from behind the curtain. "Hey, does Nana know you work at the C.S.U. Library?"

"Probably," said Bea. "Like I said, still talks to my mom."

"Hm," said Kate, realizing this meeting hadn't been a coincidence at all. She opened the door and stepped out into the night.

*

By the light of day, the abandoned unwed mothers' home took on a different air. What had been hollowed eyes and a gaping mouth became windows and a doorway with portico that had seen too many winters untended. The building was no less menacing, but its secrets felt closer to the surface—just within discovery.

Kate and Bea had decided to make the trip in the early morning hours, thinking it might be less inhabited by unsavory characters who haunted the night. They had parked a block away and braved the barren streets, walking quickly, heads down, hands in pockets.

Snow still hugged the ground as they stood outside the iron gate, but the air was warmer and quiet. A milky fog hung around the home, adding to the threat of the place.

Kate pushed on the gate, its lock holding fast. She wasn't surprised.

"We'll have to walk around," she said. "Look for another way in."

"Or at least a blind spot where we can climb over," said Bea, glancing around for prying eyes.

They walked side by side, examining the brick wall for holes, footholds, anything that might help them get to the other side. When they got to the far west corner of the property, the place where the wall curved and angled back on the edge of a ravine, they could see where it continued and was joined by a chain link fence—a second barrier between prowlers and the property.

"Let's check the other side," said Kate, turning to head back the way they had come. "Maybe that's not blocked by a ravine."

"Wait," said Bea, scanning the landscape. Kate followed her gaze, examining the land that sloped up in the distance.

"There," said Bea, pointing up into the trees that stood guard like sentinels. "Headstones."

And as Kate studied the horizon, looking between the pine trunks, she saw the slabs, aligned like scales on a dragon's back. "Lake View Cemetery?" she asked, her mind's eye trying to connect the geography.

"It's got to be," said Bea. "That's our way in."

*

As they drove under the archway to Lake View's Mayfield Road entrance, Kate and Bea stopped for a map of the nearly 30-acre cemetery. It was one of those places that everyone in Cleveland knew about, and many had even been, but most stopped at the Garfield Memorial—a castle-like structure with gargoyles toward the entrance. Beyond that landmark, the property was so massive that one could easily get lost among the graves.

Bea's Jeep took the twists and turns of the path with ease, despite the patches of ice and snow. White clung to the trees across the landscape, pale highlights on skeletal arms, haunting and beautiful. They passed ornate mausoleums, stones carved with quotes, and elaborate statues of angels, children, and loyal pets. Kate rolled down the window, removing the pane that stood between her and the dead. She breathed in the cool air, wondered about the many who were laid to rest here.

"Is it weird to love this place?" asked Bea.

"I was just thinking the same thing," said Kate.

"You remember that class picnic we took for history? Freshman year I think?" asked Bea.

"How could I forget?" Kate said. It was the summer she wanted to go into criminal investigation; she supposed snooping had always been in her blood. They had visited the grave of Eliot Ness and eaten peanut butter and jelly sandwiches on the grass nearby.

Bea snickered. "Yeah, I guess that was pretty traumatic," she said.

Kate tossed her an irritated glance. Johnny Prince had goaded her into sneaking away to see the Haserot Angel, the bronze monument with streaks like tears, then stole a kiss from her.

She learned later it was on a dare and that legend had it that any girl who was kissed there might soon die.

"Johnny Prince," Kate said. "A misogynist in the making."

"I don't recall you complaining until you found out why he did it," said Bea. She brought the Jeep to an abrupt stop, then peered through a dense network of trees.

Kate and Bea stepped out of the car without a word and walked to the edge of the cement path. Their eyes met, and they walked forward together, onto the snow and toward the crest of the hill. The land stretched out below them in ebbs and flows of trees, in crevices of ravine and stream, into pockets of light and dark.

Bea had estimated right, at least partially. They were on the edge of Lake View, but what they found was not the rooftop of the unwed mothers' home. If it was there, they couldn't see it. Rather, there was another hill that stretched out into the distance, tombstones jagged and aged.

"I don't think that's Lake View," said Bea, head tilted to the side. "That place isn't on the cemetery map."

Kate studied the stark difference between the two resting places. On one side of the tree line was cultivated earth, plants tended to by arborists, shaped and nurtured with care. On the other side, things grew wild and with abandon, untamed and untouched—maybe for decades.

"That's a lot farther than I thought it would be," said Kate.

Bea nodded. "Yeah," she said. "So, the question is, do we want to walk farther across the cemetery or go back to the front of the home and climb the wall?"

"Let's walk," said Kate, taking a step closer to the ancient resting place and Nana's footsteps. She supposed they might have to climb anyway, but scaling a chain link fence seemed a lot easier than tackling a sheer brick wall.

*

Kate stepped gingerly over the snow-covered ground, aware of the many souls at rest. The headstones were wide in variety, from pink marble to brown, grey to black, all decorated with names and relationships and dates to mark their lives. She pulled up the cowl of Nana's scarlet coat, wishing she'd brought a hat. A several mile stroll had not been on the agenda.

"I read a little about the Underground Railroad in Ohio last night," said Bea. "Stopped at the Lee Road Library on the way home from my meeting."

"Yeah?" asked Kate. "What did you find?" She watched as a hawk swirled above, searching for some breakfast. Its cry was eerie in the mist as it disappeared into the trees.

"Well, we already know Cleveland was a stop for many escaped slaves, what with Canada being so close," said Bea. "'Hope' they called it. But what I didn't realize is that University Circle was a hotbed for abolitionists."

"Interesting, considering the home isn't too far from University Circle," said Kate.

"Exactly," said Bea, breathing harder now. The ground sloped down, and it was more difficult to gain traction. "The Cozad-Bates House is in Little Italy and that's definitely recognized as part of the Underground Railroad, but that's the only one I could find officially on the record."

"Hm," said Kate, trying to keep her balance. When she looked up, Bea was staring at her, standing still.

"So," said Bea, then left it hanging in the air.

"So, what?" said Kate.

"So how do you know that house is part of the Underground Railroad?" asked Bea.

Kate had known she would have to divulge some version of the truth at some point. But she hadn't figured out how to position it yet. "Well, there's tunnels under the house."

"Okay," said Bea. "But the Underground Railroad wasn't actually underground, you realize."

Kate shrugged. "Let's keep moving," she urged, continuing down the hill. They were almost at the edge now, where a tall chain link fence divided the two cemeteries. "Just because it wasn't all underground doesn't mean that some of it might not have been."

Bea considered this for a moment. "Ok, I'll give you that. But how do you know they're there? The tunnels."

Kate sighed. She knew Bea was never going to let this go.

"Nana," she said. "Nana told me. She's seen them."

"Wait," said Bea. "Was she... Did she stay there? Like, as a patient?"

Kate stopped walking for a minute. "Don't ask me. It's not my secret to tell."

Bea held up her hands in surrender. The silence continued for some time as they approached the fence. At least there was no protective wire on top of it. It would be easy enough to climb.

"Up and over?" asked Kate. She looked at Bea, who motioned for her to go first. When she was younger this task would have been nothing. But even though Kate was in good shape, she had not hopped a fence in years.

When her feet touched down on the other side, Kate breathed heavily and shook out her hands, sore from clinging in ways to which she was no longer accustomed. And it was after a moment, after she had gotten her bearings, that she felt the eyes upon her.

Something, somewhere, was watching.

The chill crawled over her shoulders like hot breath, sending a deluge of goosebumps down her arms. She scanned the horizon, the trees, the sky. Nothing moved, not even the wind. There was a distant crow's call somewhere to the west, the low hum of a train, and even though Kate could see nothing that appeared to be a threat, she felt its presence.

Bea landed beside her, stumbled against the fence. It clanged, disturbing the silence and Kate gritted her teeth. They needed to be small, quiet.

"When did we get so old?" asked Bea, her voice ripping the air around them.

Kate turned to her and put her finger to her lips.

"When did we get so old?" Bea whispered, looking quizzically at her friend.

Kate's breath caught in her throat, and her hands began to shake. She resisted the urge to run. *How could Bea not feel this?* She thought. And she made a motion she had not in years— the hand signal for stop. The girls had taken ASL in sophomore year, and while she had forgotten much of it, there were a few things she did remember.

Bea straightened, nodded. It was a signal they only used as teenagers when something was serious. She didn't ask why, she just followed Kate as she began to jog toward the tree line.

They followed the chain link fence to the right, beyond the pine trees, searching for a place that hid them more from the elements and prying eyes. The fastest way to the home was a straight line right through the middle of the old cemetery, but instinct warned Kate against it. They finally came upon a thicket, twisting and turning with bushes and undergrowth, and they followed the growth line until they reached a place where the land sloped down.

Peering over the edge, Kate could see a small waterfall blending into a stream below. The water cut through the snow in a dark line, the white noise a welcome cover for their footsteps. They paused, looking for a way to cross.

"What happened back there?" asked Bea, her voice barely audible over the falling water.

"I don't know," said Kate. "I just felt something. Something bad."

Bea nodded, looked at her cautiously. "Like that time in Megan Wilson's attic?"

The memory rushed back at Kate, hit her in the chest. They had been foolish, playing with a Ouija board, trying to talk to ghosts. But it stopped being funny when the lights went out and the game piece started to move on its own.

"Yeah," said Kate. "Something like that."

She didn't need to say anything more. Bea didn't feel those things like she did, but she trusted her when she said there was a presence—something angry, something dangerous. It happened every so often, especially when she wasn't looking. It's what had happened at the Roxboro ravine all those years ago, when Bea had broken her arm. It had happened again at the old Church on 55th when she'd cut her ankle. Kate knew it with every fiber in her being. Bea was like a beacon for angry things, vengeful things, that had no place walking the earth.

And she realized then what a chance they were taking now.

"I have a confession to make," said Kate. "Well, two really."

Bea looked at her, waited. She rubbed her hands together, trying to warm them in their thin cotton gloves.

"Maybe this isn't safe," said Kate.

Bea smiled an impish grin. "I mean, is it ever safe when we explore?"

"I just don't want you to follow me in there and get hurt," said Kate.

"I'm a big girl, Katie. You're not dragging me anywhere against my will," said Bea.

Kate sighed. "And two," she said, pausing, knowing she had to tell her. "Those letters you sent? I never read them."

Bea's mouth opened, closed. Her brow furrowed. She turned around to the snow-covered landscape, then back to Kate.

"Not any of them?" she asked.

Kate shook her head.

"Huh," said Bea. She looked as if she'd been kicked.

"I'm sorry," said Kate. "I was—I couldn't."

"So, you don't... know anything, really," said Bea.

Kate felt shame wash over her. She bit her lip.

"Look, I'm..." began Bea. "I get that you were mad. I messed up. Over and over and I really hurt you and Nana." She sighed, threw her hands up in the air. "But there was a reason I was so lost, Katie. I told you why in those letters. I told you so that you'd understand that it wasn't just me being reckless, or… stupid."

"I'm sorry," said Kate. "I don't know what else to say."

Bea pursed her lips, searched the landscape for some type of insight. Her eyes clung to the water as it fell over the edge of the falls. "I was raped, Katie."

The words slapped Katie in the face. She stumbled back, almost fell.

"It was one of those guys from Akron I was hanging out with," said Bea.

"Bea, I—" started Kate.

"No, let me say this," Bea interrupted, looking at Kate only for a moment.

Kate nodded, swallowed. Bea's gaze returned to the waterfall.

"It left me pregnant. At 16, KK," Bea said. "There was no way I could… No way I wanted to have it. Not after…" Bea paused, shook her head. "My mom took me to get an abortion. We kept it quiet. But after, I just felt like just a piece of garbage. He took everything from me—my virginity, my first chance at being a mother. Just took it, like it meant nothing."

The tears fell freely down Bea's face now, dropping onto the snow when she looked down.

Kate moved forward. This was no time for words. She drew her arms around her old friend, squeezed her tight. Bea's body shook as she sobbed. Kate held her until the cries turned into whimpers and the whimpers into shaky breath.

"I am so sorry, Bea," whispered Kate. "For not being there for you. For not knowing. For not asking the right questions. For not reading—" Her words caught in her throat as she swallowed her own urge to cry. It was not her turn. She owed Bea this moment. "I wish I could take it back."

Bea released Kate's hug, wiped her nose with her glove.

"I should have told you when it happened. I just couldn't. I couldn't even handle it in my own mind let alone say it out loud. The only reason my mom even knew is that she figured it out, confronted me." She shook her head. "You told me not to go with them. You said you had a bad feeling. I should have listened."

"Can you forgive me?" asked Kate, the tears welling in her eyes despite her hard blinks.

Bea offered a broken smile. "No need," she said. "If I had told you, I know you would have been there for me. I pushed you away—not on purpose. I felt like a fool—you had warned me. I chose to cope in a destructive way. *I* own that—not you."

Kate raised her eyebrows. "Sounds like someone's gotten pretty wise over the last few years."

"Trying," Bea said. "Work in progress."

"Aren't we all," said Kate—a statement more than a question.

*

The air had shifted, and the sunshine peered through the clouds, its rays reflecting off the snow in a blinding white. But it felt like hope as the women searched for a safe way to navigate the sharp decline. When they located the stone stairs they stepped carefully, for while they may have once been even, the earth had skewed them over time.

The stream at the bottom was too wide and deep to cross, but a fallen tree offered passage—if they were willing to brave it. It would have been a roadblock for Kate, but Bea was not intimidated. She approached the log and mounted it like a balance beam, as Kate had seen her do many times in competition when they were younger. Gymnastics had not been Kate's thing for long, though.

"Come on," said Bea. "I know you remember how to do it."

"I stopped after year two, remember?" Kate said. She did still know how, though, even if part of her wanted to turn back. She followed as Bea scooted along the length of the tree in a straddle. Standing and walking would have ended in quick, wet misery.

By the time Kate got to the other side, Bea had already located a matching set of stone steps leading up the incline. As they climbed, the sun slipped beneath the clouds again, taking what little warmth it had to offer with it.

"We should have brought some lunch," said Bea, breathing heavily as they neared the top of the staircase.

Kate dug into her coat pocket where she found the granola bar she had stashed there before leaving Nana's that morning.

"Here," she said, handing half of it to Bea.

"Oh, nice," said Bea, devouring the bar in four bites. She had always had a ridiculous metabolism, a lanky body with an appetite of a grown man.

As they crested the top of the ravine, the land stretched out before them. Groves of trees, some still with clinging leaves, dotted the landscape. They could see the towers of the home through some of the naked branches, looming over the property. And just below them was a smaller structure with a stone façade and drooping eaves.

The chapel looked ancient, like something Kate might imagine on a European countryside—a relic of a forgotten past. The roof sagged under the snow like a melting candle, the wick a silent bell tower. The doors stood crooked on old hinges, rusted and tired from years of neglect.

The stones used to construct the walls were odd shapes—not cut rectangles, but cemented together just the way they were— all various sizes and shades of gray and brown. It was a puzzle only a stonemason could have assembled.

"Now that is something," said Bea, pulling her camera out of her coat pocket, capturing the vestige of generations past. She

walked around the ruins, leaving Kate in the hushed snow that
had begun to fall again.

Kate was glad for the silence as she stood before the chapel
doors, breathing in the cool air and the sense of peace that
invited her closer. If the cemetery land they had just crossed
was dark and foreboding, this place was its opposite. It made
her want to laugh with joy for no reason at all.

This is what churches are supposed to feel like, Kate whispered.

Kate and Bea pulled the chapel doors open together. It took
several tries to tug them ajar but finally they gave way. The
groans echoed around them until the doors stood still. And
right before Kate crossed the threshold, she felt a tingle, the
hot breath on her neck returning to yank her backwards. She
stepped forward quickly, turned to face whatever had been
hovering there, and found nothing. The snow drifted lazily
down, the landscape was still, with only her and Bea's
footprints left as breadcrumbs.

 But Bea hadn't noticed. She was already inside, walking
toward the dark alter at the other end of the chapel. As Kate's
eyes adjusted to the deep gray tones inside, she fought the
urge to shut the doors behind them. She heard a click and
light streamed from Bea's hand, illuminating the altar, the
pews, the stained-glass windows, all covered in dust that must
have been decades old.

Kate imagined a young Nana walking here, along with the
other pregnant girls. She was among their memories now.

"There's a book I'm reading," said Kate, her voice like a chant, echoing in the chapel. "Nana's book, actually."

"She wrote a book?" asked Bea, scanning the stained-glass windows with her flashlight. "I wish the light was better in here—not so good for taking pictures from the inside."

"It's a scrapbook, really. Of her time at the unwed mothers' home," said Kate, walking slowly, reverently up to the altar. She was divulging Nana's secret, but she had a feeling Nana would understand. "She wrote about this place, too."

The altar slab was barren stone. Kate grazed it with her fingers, leaving a streak in the dust that was there, taking some of it with her. Then she turned around, remembering the four-circle insignia that was supposed to be there. *Was it on the floor? On the pews?* She couldn't quite remember.

"Can I see that flashlight for a minute?" Kate asked.

Bea handed it over.

Kate searched the floor with the light then along the pews but found nothing. Then she shined the light at the altar, moved closer to study it, until she found what she was looking for.

"Here," said Kate, tracing the four connected circles on the wooden base beneath the stone slab. "This symbol is on the cover of Nana's scrapbook."

"It's a rosette," said Bea.

"A what?" asked Kate.

"Like a flower design made up of circles," said Bea. "It's one of those symbols that shows up in lots of cultures. Sometimes just designs, but also symbols of protection, associated with certain gods and goddesses. Victorians used them in gates— like the one outside this place."

Kate turned to her friend with a raised eyebrow. "Wow, you just got academic real fast."

Bea laughed. "Sorry, history nerd," she said. "It's a symbol in Christianity, too, and I'd assume that's why it's here in a church."

"Interesting, coming from you," said Kate.

Bea's family was not religious. Her mother was Jewish, and her father was raised Catholic but neither of them practiced. Religion was not a subject that had interested Bea in all the time Kate had known her. This was new.

"History of Religion course," said Bea. "Symbolism's a huge deal."

"Okay," said Kate. "So, what does it mean?"

Bea shrugged. "Maybe something to do with Jesus' wounds? I don't know if I'm remembering that right. I know the three circles represent the trinity, but I'm not sure about four."

"Well, I could have told you that," said Kate.

"I got a C. What can I say?" said Bea.

"It's on the key, too," said Kate. "That symbol."

Bea tilted her head. "Key? Key to what?"

"The passageways," she said.

"Well, do you have it? Can I see it?" asked Bea.

Kate shook her head. "No. Nana wears it on a necklace."

"Well, why didn't you ask her to borrow it? What if we need it when we get to the house?" asked Bea, putting her hands on her hips.

Kate pursed her lips. "That would make sense... if she knew we were here."

Bea rolled her eyes and sighed. "KK, if we get into the house but we can't get in..." She placed her hands on her eyes.

"I know," said Kate. "Hey, you didn't even know about the key until a minute ago..."

"But you did!" said Bea, throwing up her hands.

"I couldn't tell her. She never would have let us come," said Kate.

Bea shook her head, surrendering. "I know," she said. "But a key—I mean, that would have been good to know this morning before we drove to Lake View and walked for hours in the snow. What if it would have opened the gate in front?"

Kate should have kept her mouth shut about the key. She knew it as soon as it came out of her mouth, but it was too late now. "Well, maybe we lay the groundwork today and come back if we run into that roadblock," she said.

Bea smirked and sighed. "Deal. But you're buying coffee later. And dinner. I feel like I've earned a dinner." She walked toward the open mouth of the chapel, shaking her head. "Jesus, KK. A key," she muttered under her breath. "Anything else you forgot to tell me?"

Kate winced quietly and started to make a silent list against her will. And as the women left the chapel grounds and headed toward the main house, she looked into the woods, aware something was staring.

*

The walk to the main building took longer than they thought it would. The distance was deceptive and the accumulating snow didn't help. The back of the building was immense—a large rectangle stretching across the property, with an odd point at the far end. She remembered from her reading last night that there was supposed to be a tunnel near the oldest part of the home; she imagined a rabbit hole—a crude dirt opening with worms and other creepy-crawlies. No, she would not crawl through an opening like Alice; a door or window was much more dignified and less likely to collapse around them. Kate shuddered and examined the home's silhouette, noting the iron gate on the horizon and even more headstones beyond. It seemed like they had left the dead behind, on the other side of the ravine, but somehow the cemetery had wrapped around them in a clenching hand.

Kate and Bea went in the opposite direction of the gate, putting distance between themselves and the graveyard. They followed the length of the home then turned its sharp corner, hugging the building, looking for places to sneak inside. But there were no lower windows, as one might see on a newer house, giving access to a basement. They were almost at the front of the home when they found an entry point—a boarded up first-floor window with one of the boards pried loose. And just beneath it, a large rock upon which they could boost themselves.

Being the taller of the two, Bea went first, climbing atop the rock and prying the board away carefully. She stood silent for a moment, scanning.

"Well," said Kate. "What do you see?"

Bea turned and put her finger to her lips, motioned for Kate to join her.

"Looks like squatters have been here," said Bea. "Maybe not for some time, though." She moved aside so Kate could peer in.

She stood on her tiptoes, glancing this way and that, taking in the graffiti on the walls and discarded paper bags strewn about the floor.

"Well, I guess that's that," said Kate, turning to jump down from the rock. She had no intention of taking on squatters.

"Oh, no," said Bea. "I didn't waste all morning to get here just to leave without going in."

A nervous pang pinched Kate's stomach. But before she could protest further, Bea had pried away another board and hoisted herself up on the window ledge.

"I don't think this is a good idea," said Kate, in a harsh whisper.

But Bea was already inside.

"Shit," muttered Kate, as she clenched her teeth and followed her friend into the unknown.

They had climbed into an old study. A lone desk and a toppled chair sat in the center of the room. The trash was scattered across the desk and the floor—empty fast food bags and cigarette wrappers. Books still lined the walls, tucked in neatly, waiting to be read, but graffiti marred the spines in places. A fireplace stood cold, the remnants of an old log, partially burned, lingered below heat marks. Kate wondered how recently it had been lit.

"I bet this was the headmistress' office," said Kate. "A library of sorts."

She turned around, eyeing the walls, remembering that there should be a passage behind one of them, according to Nana's scrapbook. She settled on the only wall with no bookshelves.

Kate placed her ear close to the wall, not wanting to touch the weeping wallpaper. She raised her hand, still gloved, and knocked.

"Hollow," said Kate, feeling vindicated.

"So, the passage is behind this wall," said Bea, coming to stand beside her, eyes looking for an entry point. "Is it weird that I'm looking for a lever or something?"

Kate snorted. "Um, yeah," she said. "We're not hunting for a speakeasy."

"Ok, genius, so how do we access it?" said Bea. The sarcasm was thick in her voice.

Kate wracked her brain, trying to recall. "She mentioned lots of passages. Interconnected ones. There are two entrances I remember from the book —one in the kitchen pantry and one in the closet of their bedroom." And one outside, but she'd be damned if she was going to crawl through that.

"Kitchen pantry would be on the first floor," said Bea. "Let's look for that."

They emerged from the study into a hall, warped from time and water damage. Paint rose from the walls in scales, revealing the plaster beneath. They passed through hallway after hallway in hushed steps, careful not to wake sleeping demons or disturb floorboards that were too tired to hold their weight.

The women were led to a foyer that must have once been grand, but now lay blanketed in snow. Kate looked up through the hole in the two-story ceiling to see gray sky, dropping lazy snowflakes down onto them. A lump of ceiling remnants was unrecognizable in the center of the place; under the snow it was a contemporary sculpture, with jagged elbows and darkened crevices where the flakes could not reach. At the edges of the entrance were black and white tiles and a staircase that followed the circular enclosure up into the next level. It was the place young girls had entered the home, before they fully understood what it would cost them.

Kate's hands went to her stomach, aware of the irony in this moment. Every girl who had been here during Nana's time had little choice. No birth control, no abortion rights, some not even allowed to see their baby after birth. Kate hovered on the precipice of what she thought might be the right decision for her. There would be no going back.

Bea, oblivious of her friend's emotional turmoil, took out her camera. She began snapping photos of the snow-covered pile of debris, up at the hole in the ceiling, the snow floating down.

"This is good stuff," said Bea. "I mean, no Underground Railroad tunnels yet, but still pretty cool."

Kate looked up at Bea and she snapped the shutter, capturing her inner chaos forever.

*

When they located the kitchen area, they found it to be more intact. The cupboards, while bare, showed less damage compared to the other wing. The blue paint was chipped, but the doors still hung on their hinges in most places. Kate scanned the room and adjoining halls, looking for cupboards large enough for a person to fit. It was in the pantry hallway, an offshoot of the main kitchen, that she found her answer.

The two pantry doors opened outward and were about four feet high, just enough room for a person to squat down and enter. Kate pulled open the right door and peered inside, looking for a false panel like Nana had described. All she found was a normal backing to the cupboard, but behind the left door the paneling looked different. She knocked on it and it echoed. She turned to Bea with raised eyebrows.

"I think this is it," she said, then pushed until the panel budged.

Bea shined the light over Kate's shoulder, peering in with curiosity, as Kate crouched down, lifted the loose shelf in her way, and moved through the hole in the wall.

Kate and Bea found themselves in a passage with a dirt floor. It smelled moist and old, like pipes beneath a leaky sink. Kate covered her nose and mouth with her gloved hand, fought off a wave a nausea. She'd gone most of the day without feeling it and wished the queasiness would subside.

Bea walked first, with the light out before them like a beacon. The passage rounded to the right and led them down a staircase, where the air felt warmer and smelled more like pure earth. Kate began to breathe more quickly, like the walls were closing in around her. She stopped, gathered her courage, and struggled to keep up with her friend who seemed to have no fear.

At the bottom of the staircase was a wooden door, aged but still standing. There was a keyhole but no knob.

"This is why we needed the key," said Bea. She took out her camera to snap a photo of the door. She tossed a look back at Kate, who gasped in and out. "Hey, are you okay?"

"I think I might be claustrophobic?" Kate said—a question more than anything. "Can we go now?"

"I mean, I don't think we have a choice. I could push on the door, but that's probably a bad idea," said Bea.

"Yeah, no way," said Kate, turning around and climbing the stairs despite the dark that lay ahead of her. She had to get out. Her breath came quickly, and she felt light-headed. She had to resist the urge to run. The light bobbed as Bea followed her, up the stairs, through the dirt passage, and back through the hole in the cupboard.

When they emerged, Kate sank to the floor. She breathed deeply, trying to get her bearings.

"You alright?" asked Bea. "Did you sense something again?"

Kate shook her head. "Just good old-fashioned panic." She swallowed, wishing for some water. "That's never happened to me before."

Bea stared back at her, lips pursed, eyebrows raised.

"What?" said Kate, more irritated that she probably should be.

"Kindergarten. First sleepover," Bea said, shaking her head.

Exasperated, Kate rolled her eyes. "I was five," she said. "And it's not my fault your mom tucks the sheets in so tight. You show me any kid who wouldn't freak out getting stuck upside down in the middle of the night."

"I'm just saying that it's not the first time," Bea said, her hands in the air, waiting to catch some grace. "That was pretty cool, though. Being in that tunnel. Thinking about all the people who might have walked through it."

"Yeah," said Kate. "Real cool."

She would think so later, she knew, but right now while the panic was still subsiding and her stomach was trying to unknot itself, all she wanted was to be at Nana's on the couch tucked in under a blanket—right side up.

"Well, I say we head back. I'm starving, and you're buying," said Bea.

"Yeah, yeah," said Kate, following her back through the home and out the way they had come in.

*

As Kate emerged from the study window and onto the rock, she thought she saw something move in the trees toward the front of the property. She examined the landscape as Bea climbed out then down to stand beside her.

"I could swear I just saw something move over there," said Kate.

"We need to go check that perimeter of the brick wall anyway," said Bea. "Maybe there's an easier way in."

Bea started walking toward the wall, but Kate lagged behind, something repelling her.

"Hey, Bea?" said Kate, in an attempt to warn her, but she was already too far away to hear.

When they reached the wall, the place Kate thought she had seen movement, what they found made them both groan in frustration. The hole there was just large enough for both of them to squeeze through.

"We literally walked all that way from Lake View for nothing," said Bea, throwing her hands up in the air. "Oh, my god. I'm so annoyed."

"Well," said Kate, "at least we got to see the chapel, right?" She wasn't about to remind Bea that it had been her idea to go in through the back.

Bea tossed her an irritated glance.

"Yeah, we'll see if you're still looking on the bright side by the time we get back to the car." She offered an ironic smile, then began the long trek back through the back of the property and across the cemetery.

Kate shook her head, knowing Bea was right. As if to add insult, her stomach growled loudly, no longer subdued by nausea. Before she followed her friend, though, she stood at the hole in the wall—waiting for what, she wasn't sure.

Something lingered there—a scent on the air. A musk that made Kate's nose wrinkle and her ears perk. And then it was gone, swept away in the cold swirl of snowflakes in the ebbing afternoon sun. Kate turned her back and followed her friend through the footsteps that had led them there.

*

Kate had always believed the truth was important. She'd waved this banner even in the throws of her adolescent years, erring on the side of honesty unless it would hurt someone too much. Despite her dislike of religious dogma, she did have a very strong moral compass—one that pestered her if it was ignored or violated in any way. But the past two months had been a sharp departure from the inner sense that had long been her guide.

She had lost her way.

It was this awareness that hung over her like a storm cloud at the Thanksgiving dinner table. She wanted to focus on things to be thankful for—her family, her education, her health. Gratitude always brought feelings of reassurance, contentment, hope. Having her body hijacked by something she never asked for, though, was a kind of trap she'd not experienced before. Everywhere she went, the problem followed.

It grew inside her, stealing her nutrients, barring her from any relief in the form of alcohol or nicotine, tying her forever to a man she barely knew. The thoughts spiraled, pulling her down a deep, dark hole that swirled into nothingness, dragging her with it.

"The turkey alright?" asked Nana, watching Kate sit there with chaos threatening to eat her from the inside out. She was wearing an elegant, red velvet blouse with a scooped neck—a style not many older women could pull off. But Nana had a timelessness about her and where others had wrinkles and folds, she merely had lines. She fingered the lone pendant that hung there—a sapphire Grandfather had bought her right before he passed.

Kate smiled, tried to look grateful. "It's wonderful, Nana. Thank you."

Wonderful. Wonderfully thoughtful and giving and a constant positive presence in Kate's life. That's what Nana was—an angel in every sense of the word. Yet here Kate was, not telling her they had visited the unwed mothers' home just the day before. She drew a shaky breath, stuck her fork into the mound of mashed potatoes and pit of gravy. The pepper danced on top, clung to the portion she placed in her mouth.

"So," said Nana. "Tell me how it was seeing Bea again." Her knowing smile hinted at the ulterior motive she'd had, sending Kate to the C.S.U. Library.

"It was good," said Kate, not wanting to call Nana out. She sighed. "Despite everything, she's still the same old Bea." She looked down at her plate. "I don't think I've been a very good friend since I lost her. Like it broke part of me, maybe. I think it's why I…" She motioned to her stomach, but her throat constricted again and the tears spilled over the edge.

Nana put down her fork, put her hand on Kate's. She simply breathed with her until the tears subsided.

"Bea said," said Kate, "There were reasons she got high—reasons she shared with me in letters that I never read. She trusted me with her secrets—she reached out. But I didn't... How could I do that?"

"Honey, you didn't know," said Nana.

"I was so mad at her after the funeral," said Kate. "She took that day from me—from us."

"She was grieving, too," said Nana. "Don't forget that he was like a grandfather for her also. Pain makes people do crazy things. Things they wouldn't normally do."

Kate nodded. "Like sleep with their roommate's boyfriend?"

"Mm-hm," mumbled Nana. "Something like that." She didn't ask, and Kate didn't explain.

*

Kate was thankful she was more composed by the time Bea rang the doorbell for dessert. Watching her hug Nana felt like a mending of sorts, bringing together pieces of a puzzle long forgotten. And without any prodding, Nana gave her permission to share the scrapbook with Bea, so they poured over it for hours, even after Nana had gone to bed.

"We've got to go back tomorrow," said Bea, her eyes glowing from the detail in the scrapbook. "Don't you want to open that door in the tunnel? Check out the other passages? Maybe look more carefully through that study to see if we can find any records?"

Kate nodded, though the thought of going back into the passage behind the pantry made her muscles go rigid. "Well, we're not opening that door without the key," she said. "And there's no way Nana will give it to us."

Bea paused, licked her lips, preparing her defense.

"KK, documenting an Underground Railroad discovery could be incredible for my thesis," said Bea. "And writing about it could be really good for your work, too! And then there's the whole historical aspect of the unwed mothers' home itself. It's like the universe has just dropped this gift into our laps, you know?"

Bea finally stopped her impassioned plea long enough to see that Kate was not as enthused.

"What?" she said, taking a breath. "What's wrong?"

"I don't like keeping this from Nana," said Kate.

Bea nodded. "I get that, but she'd never let us go. Not to that neighborhood. Not alone."

"I know," said Kate. "It's why I haven't said anything to her yet."

"Do you not want to go?" asked Bea. Her eyes were pleading.

"Of course I want to go," said Kate. "It's why I dragged you with me in the first place. I just don't like lying about it. I'm starting to feel like a horrible person."

"Okay," said Bea. "One more day. Just one. And then we'll tell her. If I can document just a little more, maybe I can appeal to the school and they'll help me get whatever paperwork I need to study it further—with a team. Maybe apply for a grant. And, with you—if you're willing. I would never do that without asking you."

Kate nodded. She *was* curious. And she was interested in studying the place—not just exploring, but really digging into its history, its stories. There was so much she could write about.

"One more day, then no more secrets," she said.

*

The next day, Kate and Bea went back to the abandoned home for unwed mothers. They parked on Euclid, on the furthest edges of the Case Western Reserve University property, and walked the rest of the way. The wind was colder, sharper, like a warning as it slapped Kate's cheeks. She tucked her chin down into Nana's red scarf and pulled at its matching cap so that her ears were safely wrapped in warmth.

They passed by abandoned buildings and boarded up shops. And while some were still open, no one huddled in doorways or passed them on the street. The bitter cold had scared them all inside. Bea and Kate had only the bluster whistling past them for company.

"Don't be mad," said Bea. They had just climbed through the hole in the brick wall and stood outside of the home, on the precipice of another adventure.

Kate's insides tensed—she knew that tone in Bea's voice. It reeked of mischief for which Kate hadn't bargained. The whole "better to ask forgiveness than permission" notion was baked into Bea's eyes.

Kate sighed, her breath floating up into the gray sky like smoke behind the protective brick wall. "I'm afraid to ask," she said.

From around her neck, Bea revealed the key. *Nana's* key.

The anger flared in Kate's chest. "Did she give that to you?" she said, knowing it wasn't the case.

"I borrowed it," said Bea, already prepared to dive into an explanation.

"Stole it," said Kate. "You *stole* it."

"No," said Bea. "I just borrowed. Just for today. If we unlock the door, we can leave it unlocked. Problem solved. The key will be back safe with Nana tonight."

Anger simmered in Kate's head. It was already done, though. And here they were, standing in front of the home. She put her hands over her face.

"Damn it, Bea," Kate said.

"I know, I'm sorry, I just…" Bea said, stammering. "It's right in front of us, Katie, right there! And when I saw she wasn't wearing it last night… And then it was on the sink in the bathroom…"

Kate looked at Bea with irony. "It just jumped into your hands and into your pocket."

Bea shrugged, her eyes wide with excitement. "It'll be like it never happened," she said. "We go home, you put it back."

"No, *you* put it back," said Kate. "If I put it back, it's going into Nana's hand. And what makes you think she hasn't missed it already?"

"Did she mention it to you this morning?" asked Bea.

"Well, no," said Kate. "But that doesn't make it right."

"I'm okay with not being right," said Bea. "I'm not okay with walking away from what's on the other side of that door."

In truth, Kate wasn't either, but she was not about to say it.

"You never would have taken it," said Bea, her voice quieter now.

She was right. "*You're* putting it back—tonight," said Kate.

Bea nodded, and they walked toward the house in silence.

*

Kate knew what she was in for as they went through the hole behind the pantry door, but it did nothing to stave off the panic that threatened to erupt. She moved quickly behind Bea, determined to see this through one more time, keeping her mind focused on the keyhole. One turn and they would know. They would see.

When they reached the bottom of the stairs, she held the flashlight and shined it on the door for Bea, who fumbled with the key. The light danced in her hand, nerves that refused to calm despite careful, conscious breaths.

"It won't turn," said Bea. She pulled the key out, huffed, placed it in the lock again. "Wait," she said. And then there was a click.

Bea pushed the door open to reveal a small room. An aged smell Kate could not quite place wafted toward her—of dust and earth and time. She coughed, drew her scarf over her mouth. Bea took the flashlight from her, scanned the space with it, revealing three other doors located at cardinal points around the room. Much of it was what she had pictured from Nana's words, but there was a dungeon-like feeling about the place that was more tangible as she stood there on the threshold.

Something told her not to go inside.

"I can't be here," she whispered.

"Ok," said Bea, "just let me check those doors, see if they need a key. Hold this." She placed the flashlight back in her friend's hand.

Kate fought unease and tried to hold the light steady, though it bobbed in rhythmic jumps on the walls. Bea clicked one door and moved to the next, and it was as the light followed her that Kate saw the box in the center of the room. It was a rectangular wooden box with a carved top.

"Hey," said Bea. "Light, KK."

Kate moved the light back to the second door, and Bea clicked that one, too. Kate's eyes went back to the box, its small shape barely a shadow on the uneven stone floor.

She wanted to get that box. No, she *needed* to.

But as Kate crossed the threshold into the room, she shrank with a sickening repulsion. Her knees began to shake and a wallowing sadness took root in her chest that seemed to spread down her arms, her legs, engulfing her.

Kate backed up, trying to maintain her presence for Bea's sake, fighting the urge to run. The walls closed in on her, then expanded, like they were breathing. The disquiet grew, crawling up her back, sitting on her chest, wrapping around her throat.

Something did not want them down there.

Bea moved to the third door, fiddled with the key, and finally there was a click.

"Get the box. On the floor," said Kate, backing up. "We need to get out. Now." The panic spilled over into her stomach, and Kate hurled. Once, twice. She gasped as she turned toward the stairs.

"Bea!" she squeaked out between breaths, trying not to gag on the taste of vomit.

And then Bea was beside her, pulling her up off the floor, up the stairs.

"The box," she whispered.

"Got it," said Bea, one arm tight around her friend, the other clutching the box.

When they made it safely through the pantry door, Kate sank to her knees. Never in her whole life had she felt this way. It was more than a panic attack, more than morning sickness, so much more. There were no words to capture the menace she felt chasing them up the stairs.

It was hatred. A deep, dark malice for their very existence. Something biting at their feet as they ran, reaching out like a whip to break their skin and suck juices out from the wounds. But it was stuck behind the panel in the cupboard—for now.

"Are you ok?" asked Bea, setting the box down on the counter.

Kate shook her head. "We need to get out of here," she said.

"It's just a panic attack," said Bea. "It's okay, just stay up here. Let me just go get some pictures. The doors are already unlocked. You don't have to come back down with me."

"No!" yelled Kate. "We need to get out of here now!" It was almost a scream.

Bea's eyes widened with surprise.

"Jesus, Katie," said Bea.

Kate rose to her feet, quieted her voice. "You're not hearing me. It's not safe, Bea. Something's down there. You can't go back—not by yourself. Not now."

Bea nodded. Her mouth opened, closed. No words came out. "Okay, we'll go," she said.

It was when they turned toward the hall to go back toward the study, toward the window and freedom, that they saw the man.

He was a dark silhouette, tall with large shoulders. His hair was wild, unkempt. His clothing haggard. His face disappeared into a grizzly beard that only moved when he let out one, long, guttural cry. He was upon Kate before she had a chance to run.

Iron arms clamped around her body. She was pinned to the wall with a crack. Her vision blurred. She couldn't breathe. Couldn't move. But she fought. Pushing, pressing, biting. She kicked his legs, over and over. The grip loosened. The smell of urine was strong in her nose. The taste of blood metallic in her mouth. She brought her knee up to his groin area in a thrust.

Bea was somewhere in the mix—Kate could smell her apple hair sullied with his stink. The man backed away, clutching his stomach. But he was still blocking the door. A click. The flash of a knife.

"Not her!" screamed Bea. "She's pregnant. Me! You want me!"

He turned to Bea, cocked his head, advanced in her direction.

Kate scanned the room for a weapon—anything. She picked up the wooden box and hit him in the back of the head. It bounced off, landed on the floor. He turned back to her, his face a tangle of fury and teeth and fur.

The beast lunged and everything went dark.

*

She has seen the wolf.

These words echo in Kate's mind, ricocheting off the curves of her skull, gaining momentum. She winced. The pain seared, throbbed, ushered nausea. *Shut up,* Kate thought. But her mind would not listen. And through the fog of half consciousness, she heard her own voice whisper: *She has seen the man.*

Ursula K. Le Guin had it right in "The Wife's Story," that the tales of "Little Red Riding Hood" got it wrong, that it was man who should be feared all along. Maybe Kate was the wolf. Wolves mate for life. They are part of a pack. They take only what they need, and they care for each other. But humans don't function that way. Humans take what they want. Especially bad men. They take and take and take.

As Kate slipped beneath awareness, she found herself in a maze, a labyrinth. The walls seemed to close in around her, giving her only two ways to run—back or forward. Her thumb and forefinger gripped tightly to the candleholder, and she was careful not to let any wax fall onto her skin. The golden glow was eaten by the air; it illuminated little and left her mostly in the dark. It was a spotlight, revealing her to anything lurking behind the next turn.

Her bare feet scraped along the dirt path, the random jagged stone reaching out to prick her, daring her to stumble. She could hear the trickling of water somewhere in the distance. Should she move toward it or run away? The ceiling above was uneven, roots dangling like bony hands. She was underground.

At the thought Kate began to panic. She had to get out. She had to get out!

When she looked at the candle again, it was much lower, impossibly lower, disappearing with every breath. She looked around, feeling suffocated by the walls. It was then that she saw the eyes glowing in the darkness—coming from the trail behind her.

She froze. Gasped.

Her muscles went rigid with panic. She ran.

She could hear the thing breathing behind her, its heat reaching out to inhale her, devour her. Faster, faster!

The growl was behind her.

A slice on her arm.

A scream.

And the light went out.

*

Kate's eyes fluttered open. The world was dark and gray, with pale streams of faint light reaching in from under a closed door. Her hands were bound at the wrists, but she could roll over. Her ankles were bound, too, like an animal prepared for slaughter. Her mouth wasn't gagged. She opened it to scream, then snapped it shut. No, that could be bad for Bea. If she was still alive. Her breath caught in her throat.

Bea.

Kate needed to get her bearings—quietly.

She was on the floor of the study in the unwed mothers' home. As her eyes adjusted to the dimness, she could see the books tucked into their places on the shelves. The boarded-up window that had granted them entry was now covered completely.

Kate strained her ears. She listened for voices, cries, screams. There was wind whistling in ebbs and flows through the bare branches, a dog barking in the far distance, a rumbling like a train a block or two away. Bea's face came rushing into her mind's eye—the look in her eyes as she tried to tempt the man in her direction, away from Kate. As she put herself on the altar of that man's—that beast's—appetite.

The tears stung her eyes, and her body began to shake. *Pull it together, Kate*, she whispered through gritted teeth. There was no room for mistakes now. No room for letting panic dictate her next move. She inhaled slowly, exhaled, inhaled again.

She wriggled her hands, testing the strength of the binding. There was some give, but not much. At least he had tied them in front and not behind her.

At least there was that.

She sat up, tested her ankle ties, which were looser. Curling her knees to her chest, Kate was able to reach the twine, its texture rough under her fingers. She found the knot, pinched at it with her fingers, pulled at it with her nails. She worked the knot until her fingers were raw. And finally, it gave.

She stood, dizziness swirling around her, until she leaned onto the desk for support. The pain ripped through her head, one throb, then two, and finally a dull ache that descended into a high-pitched squeal. Then silence.

Kate looked toward the boarded window, considered going for help. But help might not be close. *It might already be too late,* she thought. Her eyes scanned the dim room and landed on the poker beside the fireplace. It lay in a stand with a broom, forgotten and collecting dust. She hoped it would do. She would not go down without a fight and she'd be damned if she left Bea to the claws of fate.

Armed with her makeshift weapon, Kate crept toward the closed door and put her ear to it. The home groaned like it was alive, but there was no trace of voices or movement. She opened the door slowly, carefully, holding her breath despite her racing heart. Anger burned in her chest, and she let it, eclipsing the fear that nagged around the edges.

She made her way down the maze of hallways, through the entry hall, to the place where it happened—to the place where Bea… Kate steeled herself from what she might find. A barrage of images struck her—Bea on the floor. Bea fighting him off. Bea splayed open. Kate squeezed her eyes shut, clenched her teeth, tightened her grip on the poker. Its metal was cold in her hand, stinging and sharp. She felt its weight, gauged its length, prepared to swing.

But the pantry was abandoned. It was a tableau, an aged kitchen under a layer of dust, painted in the dim light of winter evening that peeked in through cracks in the boarded windows. *Where would he have taken her?* Kate searched the recesses of her memory for what she knew about criminals, wishing she'd had more than a minor in psych. *Comfort zone,* she thought. He would likely take her to what was familiar—in this house or out of it. Leaving would be too risky, especially if he was squatting in this building. *They must be here.*

Kate tossed over the description Nana had provided in the book. Their boarding room in one wing, the second floor if she remembered right. Then there was a hospital wing, the place they delivered the babies—a third floor maybe? The boarding rooms might feel more like home, she decided, and prepared to ascend the staircase that led from the entry hall to the second floor.

Moonlight spilled into the foyer from the hole in the ceiling, revealing footprints in the snow on black and white floor. She took the stairs slowly, for they groaned beneath her weight, even under a layer of old carpet. The closer Kate got to the top of the stairs, the more rigid her body became. Her hands shook, her legs quivered, but she stayed focused on her goal— *get to Bea.*

Just as she was about to round the corner to the first hallway on the left, Kate heard something. She paused, waiting, strained her ears. And there it was again—a muffled sob. *Bea.* She wasn't far. Just down the hall.

Kate peered around the bend. The hallway was empty except for a lone stroller, sitting still in the middle of the hall like it had been waiting for a baby all this time. She placed her feet carefully, closing the distance between her and the first room on the left, where the door was closed.

A harsh light shone from underneath the door, flickering with shadow, hinting at movement. Someone passed by the door once, again.

And Kate got an idea.

She grasped the handle of the baby stroller, shifted it. It retorted with a rusty squeak. There was a rustle from within the room, stomping feet. When the door opened, she gave the stroller a push, sending it rolling down the hallway. And he appeared, glancing first at the pram, and then turned toward Kate.

She grasped the poker with both hands and swung with every ounce of her being. It hit his face with a crack, sending him stumbling backwards into the room. Kate advanced, ready to swing again. He lay howling on the floor, hands over face, trying to hold in the blood. It seeped through his fingers in spurts, in time with his heartbeat.

Bea jumped to her feet, clothes half on, half off. The key hung between her bare breasts, swinging back and forth like a pendulum as she leapt for the door. Her face was contorted in anger and pain, blood at the corner of her mouth, tears wet on her cheeks, snot running from her nose.

They ran. Down the stairs and to the front door. Kate pushed and turned the handle but there was no give. Pounding feet were chasing them, running down the stairs. Then he was tumbling, tumbling toward them. He landed with a crash into the front door, where he slumped.

Bea led the way, down the hall and to the study. Kate took the poker to the boards, sending wood chips flying. Bea held up her hands, and Kate stopped. Bea kicked at the remaining boards, and Kate shut the study door, pushed the old desk up against it. It might not stop him for long.

Kate turned to see Bea disappearing through the window as a thud struck the closed study door. Kate dropped the poker, picked up the wooden box with the carved lid, and squeezed through the window. She dropped to the rock below just in time to see him come through the study door.

They ran through the snow, Bea pulling her shirt on as they ran. Her jacket had been left behind with all of their foolish curiosity. And as they knelt and crawled through the hole in the brick wall, Kate thought she could hear the gnashing of teeth, a low guttural growl. Closer, closer.

On the other side of the wall, they emerged in the glow of streetlights—Alices tumbling out of the rabbit hole. Kate snuck one more glance behind them as they ran, breath like smoke, box clutched to her chest, and all she found was a quiet street.

The beast was gone.

*

When the police arrested the homeless man who was squatting in the home for unwed mothers, they found no prior arrests. The news reported the attack on two girls who were "urban exploring," as the journalist put it, and they interviewed other homeless people in the area who claimed to know the perpetrator.

He was never violent, said one associate. *The nicest guy, but usually drunk,* said another. *Would give you the shirt off his back. That's the way we do it here—take care of each other.* None of these things matched up with the ferociousness they had seen.

But Kate knew.

She had seen the wolf.

The Wolf.

It was a dark presence that lingered around the home, a memory of a man long dead who clung to the evil that infected the walls, the carpet, the floorboards. Like a subterranean river snaking beneath the house, he bled into the very soil Prescott House stood upon. And he had inhabited the squatter's body—a vessel through which he could move in the waking world.

Nana had said The Wolf was not Kate's ghost. And it had not been before. But things had changed. *She* had changed. She would never unsee his bared teeth, never unfeel the malice that reached out to choke her. The unease shuddered through her even as she sat in Nana's kitchen, safe behind walls that had always felt like home.

Chills rose on Kate's arms, but she did not look away from the wolf in the painting on the wall. The two golden disks glared, but their magic had been punctured. Her eyes drifted to the little girl in red, and the basket she held. No longer did her pose seem defensive. *No*, thought Kate, *she is protecting that basket.* Protecting all things feminine from the wolves of this world.

Kate thought of Nana as the young girl abandoned to an unwed mothers' home to hide her shame. She thought of the friends she made, the hope she found, and the story that ultimately led Kate back to her own estranged sister. Her Bea.

Maybe "Little Red Riding Hood" was not only a warning for young girls. Of pins and needles. Of virginity and maidenhood. Of men who might steal their innocence. Maybe it was also a story of discovery—of knowing the power of motherhood, and grandmotherhood, and finding one's own voice.

The power to *choose*.

And as she sat at Nana's table, in her warm kitchen, with a cup of Café Du Monde and a pen in her hand, she began to write. *Her* version of the story.

This is a new short story created for this collection, but it is connected to the author's novel, *The Butterfly Circle*, which tells Nana's story at the unwed mothers' home in 1948. The box referred to in this short story belongs to Nana and her friends, which is detailed in the novel. The novel is available at libraries, bookstores, and online retailers.

Works Cited

Carter, Angela. "The Company of Wolves." *The Bloody Chamber*, Penguin Books, 1979, pp. 141-152.

Roots in the Cove: A Modern Fairy Tale

Smoky Mountains, U.S.A.

Sunday Morning.

James woke on the cabin floor. The smell of pine filled his nose and an ache like a dagger split his frontal lobe. As the world came back into focus and memory flooded over him, he sat up quickly.

Was he alone?

Was the creature gone?

He leapt to his feet, staggered, caught himself on a kitchen chair. He'd either drunken himself insane or last night was real. He glanced around, gingerly touched his forehead. It was sticky, red when he pulled his hand away. He moved toward the back door that stood ajar, afraid of what he might find.

This wasn't how this weekend was supposed to go.

*

Last Thursday

The Great Smoky Mountains loomed in the distance, their silhouettes rising into the sky like frozen tidal waves, dark against a blue backdrop. A white cloud rolled overhead, casting a shadow that crawled across grass and trees like an impending monster. Veronica held her breath as it passed over her, and James reached for her hand, but she didn't notice. His fingers found hers and she received them, but did not tear her gaze from the landscape.

She was like that sometimes—dreamily lost in a place where he couldn't quite find her.

"Thinking about our wedding?" James asked, almost afraid to break the spell the mountains had cast on her.

"Yeah," she whispered, glanced at him slowly. "I'm excited to announce the engagement."

Her eyes were pools of chocolate.

"Good, let's go get that selfie by the falls," he urged, but her gaze was back in the distance like a fly caught in honey. "We'll post it tonight."

She nodded slowly, then smiled back at him and pulled herself away from the picturesque scene. It dragged after her like gum on a shoe.

They cleaned up the remains of the lunch they had eaten at the picnic area and tossed the garbage into bins that warned: clean up waste—bears will pillage.

*

It was dusk by the time they pulled away from Laurel Falls and drove toward the vacation cabin. Google said it was several miles away, but the sun fell fast, its last rays sinking below the horizon, leaving them with only their headlights as guides. The darkness was thick on either side of the road and the land grew murkier as they climbed in elevation.

James felt disoriented by the change in topography. The road was the rim of a glass—if they veered off course, they would plummet down either side. It twisted and turned, mist played with the light, reflecting it back to them as they drove higher, higher. They ticked up the rollercoaster, the front of the vehicle on a sharp incline. Veronica's breath quickened; her anxiety grew by the minute. It had been a mistake to wait until dark to head to the cabin.

"Are we almost there?" she asked with a shaky voice.

"Almost." The discomfort was growing in him, too, but he wouldn't let it show. "Watch for a sign that says Cave Road, then we want number 25."

The road leveled out where they found their turn, but sloped back up to an incline sharply. Heading east, they passed driveways with signs in the teens that alternated on the left and the right. No cabins were visible—they were set back too far with no lights, no sign of humanity. They might as well have been in a tunnel underground. And then there it was, a carved 25 on a wooden sign, marking the driveway to their rented home.

James guided the front end of the Trailblazer down the rocky path, which was longer than he anticipated. Headlights illuminated the front of a rustic cabin nestled among trees that formed a canopy above. Only a small section of sky was visible above the roof, speckled with stars.

He pulled alongside the cabin where the driveway came to an end. Veronica gasped as the car went over a bump, began a sharp decline. The night was an optical illusion; they hadn't expected the change in inclination. James slammed on the brakes, coins that had been in the cupholder spilling all over the floor. He put the car into park as they caught their breath, looked down into the thick woods illuminated by headlights. Mist gathered among the trunks. Were they above the clouds or had the clouds descended to meet them?

"I think I almost had a heart attack," whispered Veronica between breaths.

"Same," said James, then he laughed apprehensively, hoping it would ease her nerves.

They headed up a short staircase to the front door, Veronica almost on top of him.

"Honey, it's just the dark," he said, clicking the flashlight app on his phone, handing it to her so that he could enter the code to the lockbox that held the cabin key.

"You saw those warning signs at the park." Her hands were shaking as she held the cell phone. "There are bears."

"Oh my!" he said without missing a beat. He could see her smirk in the glow of the phone. The lockbox popped open and the key was in his hand. "You go inside and check it out—I'll get our things."

"No argument here," she said, stepping into the cabin, flipping on the lights. A yellow glow flooded out from the windows as he trekked back and forth to the car, unloading their bags.

By the time he closed the door for the night, Veronica had settled at the kitchen counter with a glass of merlot; she stared out the back window, lost in thought. He scanned the first floor of the cabin as he slowly moved toward her, taking in their rental.

Rich pine walls surrounded them on all sides except for the windows. The open floorplan included a living room and kitchen that flowed seamlessly into one another, with columns made of intact trees supporting the two-story roof that loomed over the living room. There was a full bath on the first floor and a staircase that led to a loft bedroom above the kitchen. The rustic railing was made of crooked twigs—right out of a storybook. He ran his hand over a column of smooth wood as he entered the kitchen, felt where the knots had once held branches. The cabin was the work of a craftsman.

His eyes settled on Veronica, still lost in her stare. He followed her gaze, seeing only the dark that lay beyond the picture window. It took him a moment to notice the small white moths gathered there, like miniature angels. Their wings were pure and shiny in the light, their underbellies visible through the glass.

James wrapped his arms around his fiancé, feeling her warmth against him. She relaxed into his arms for a moment, her breath steady and calming.

"I can't wait till we have kids and can share this with them," he said.

She mumbled in agreement, but wriggled out of his embrace, quietly walked to the window with her finger outstretched. She moved slowly, as if her presence would frighten the moths, but they were still—flowers resting on a puddle and Veronica beneath its surface. Her finger connected with the glass like she could capture some of their magic, but her movement was a rock tossed into still water; the flowers took off into the night. They were in another realm—beyond her reach.

"Hon, I'm beat," he said, stifling a yawn. "Mind if I head upstairs to bed?"

She glanced back at him, her dark hair hanging softly around her face—his angel.

"Nope," she said. "I might just enjoy the quiet for a little while. Be up soon."

He kissed her on the forehead and headed toward the stairs, too tired to lug a suitcase behind him. It would wait until morning.

"Don't drink too much," he muttered, as he tried to find his way in the dim loft.

*

James lay still beside his fiancé, his chest rising and falling in a smooth pattern. Veronica danced on the fringes of sleep, lulled by the rhythmic plunking of rain on the cabin roof, a patchwork quilt tucked gently under her chin. As she fell deeper into relaxation and began to dream, a hum arose somewhere in the dark, seeping into the bedroom through a cracked window. It drifted on thick air, calling to her. Her subconscious crawled out of bed after it, followed it across the floor on tiptoes, chased it down the stairs to the back door.

Then she woke.

She lay on the expansive porch at the back of the cabin, the glass door cracked open behind her. The night air swept through her hair, tickled her face, chilled her bare shoulders. The nightgown she wore was drenched with sweat, the spaghetti straps barely hanging on to her small frame under its weight. Alarmed, she staggered to her feet and quietly snuck back inside.

Had she had that much to drink?

James had said not to.

As the door clicked shut, she locked the handle, backed away as if it might open on its own. Shame filled her, wrapped itself around her like a blanket as she crept back into bed.

*

Friday

"Eleven a.m. and we already have 100 likes." Veronica's smile was bright and cheery as she sat in the passenger seat of the Trailblazer. James wasn't surprised she was having fun posting their engagement announcement on Instagram. The pressure her family had put on her to get married had been constant for the last few years; she'd sighed with relief when the post had been made and then called her mother to deliver the good news.

He knew Veronica loved him, but part of him wondered if she'd said yes just to quell her mother's hounding. He decided that accusation might not go over well, swallowed the emotion that grew in his throat, and it sank into his stomach like a rock.

Veronica read from the pamphlet they had found in the cabin, the one that had brought them on this driving tour in the first place.

"It says here this land was once Cherokee territory, then European settlers came. A town was here for over a hundred years, but then the government purchased the land in 1945." She paused, gulped. "I wonder how amenable those families were to that transaction?"

James smirked and sarcasm filled his voice. "The government taking something without permission? Ha. Imagine that." He huffed. "At least they got paid, I doubt the Indians got that much."

Veronica pursed her lips, wondering if they were trespassing on sacred ground. She imagined echoes of the past beneath the surface, lingering, waiting for someone to find them like lost change. Her mother had said they had family ties to the Smoky Mountains, but didn't know more than that. She envisioned a woman from the past driving in a covered wagon, her husband beside her. It would have been a hard life—no electricity, harsh winters, growing your own food. And the lack of choices, too—wife or school teacher at best… no birth control.

She shuddered.

As they pulled onto the path for the "driving tour" at Cades Cove, an odd feeling crept over both of them. James put his hand to his head, scratched, felt like there was something he'd forgotten that was trying to find its way back to him. Veronica was overcome with emotion; the scenery was captivating, but there was something more, something underneath the layer of reality before them. It tugged at the wisps of hair around her face, brushed against her skin like hot breath, tingled her spine in recognition of coming home. But she couldn't capture these feelings in words so she said nothing.

They followed signs that said "10 miles per hour," "remain in your vehicle," and "no stopping for pictures." The train of cars before them and behind was long, but they didn't notice. Perhaps everyone was just as mesmerized.

They drove along in silence, following the road that encircled the park, a peaceful feeling finally enveloping the couple. They were lulled by the butterflies dancing in sunbeams, the golden light magical. The trees there grew from underneath a lazy river, roots spreading from little islands, disappearing beneath the water to another world.

Around a bend the landscape changed. The winding river disappeared, replaced by a pasture that stretched for miles, surrounded by immense mountains on all sides. They were in the heart of a valley that felt ancient, and despite the hum of engines nearby, a hush settled in the air. Pioneer ruins rose in the distance, their roofs filling the holler. Echoes of people who once lived there lingered in the rustling leaves of sugar maples.

Then the cars came to an abrupt stop. They could see people getting out of their vehicles, pulling out cameras, moving closer to the edge of the path and closer to the woods that sloped into mountains. James put the car in park, huffed in frustration.

"Clearly they didn't see the signs," he began, irritation in his voice.

But Veronica grabbed her cell phone, opened the door and followed them.

"Hey! What are you doing? Veronica!" he called, but she ignored him.

Her eyes focused on the dark shape among the trees, slowly lurching back and forth as it walked. The bear's fur was a deep brown, and she might not have seen her if others hadn't noticed first. Then there was a smaller shape, bounding down a tree with agile movements.

A cub!

Veronica's heart swelled.

She tapped her screen, opened the camera, and aimed. *Click.*

There was more movement—another cub, and yet another. The three little ones followed her mother, sauntering away from the crowd all in a row. *Click.*

"Return to your cars!" The voice boomed over a megaphone.

Veronica turned to see a park ranger approaching on horseback. "For your safety and the bears' return to your cars now!"

Then James was beside her, clutching her wrist.

"Come on," he said, the anger in his voice clear. "Get in the car."

She followed after him, resisting his grip that only grew tighter.

"I don't know what you were thinking," he muttered once they were safe inside the car.

"I just wanted to see what the deal was," she said, hurt at his patronizing tone.

"Well, it was stupid," he said.

Veronica's eyes remained on her phone, and she scrolled through the pictures she'd taken. The three babies following their mother were wild and free.

Magical.

"Look," said James, touching her arm gingerly. "The signs are there for a reason. We need to heed them."

Veronica nodded so that he would stop talking at her.

*

When James woke and felt the empty space next to him, he sat up in bed. Had Veronica even come to bed? He'd left her downstairs with an open bottle of wine, still stewing about the argument they had over dinner.

He didn't see what the big deal was. She wanted a tattoo. He didn't want her to get one. She was going to be his bride—the mother of his children. They were becoming *one*. He wouldn't just mark up his body without consulting her and she owed him the same courtesy. He thought they were trashy. Why ruin something so perfect? He'd said. She hadn't taken it as a compliment.

The light from downstairs filtered in through the cracked door, seeping into the bedroom like a beacon. He'd better go check on her. There was no telling how long this tantrum of hers would last. Veronica was stubborn. He'd figured that out early in their relationship. If she was determined to do something, there was little he could do to stop her. He was hoping that would change with time, as they settled into their lives and had kids.

James pulled on a T-shirt and wiped the sleep from his eyes as he made his way down the storybook stairs. They creaked under his weight—a cozy sound that reminded him of childhood. He hoped that one day they would have their own creaky stairs and stories about the children who climbed them. Maybe they would sneak down on Christmas morning to catch a glimpse of Santa.

"Hon?" he called out. "Veronica?"

Silence filled the two-story living room like a heavy weight. He turned the corner and fully expected to find her at the kitchen table, still nursing a glass of wine. But the glass sat there alone, the remnants of merlot a small puddle, like tears in a snow globe. The back door stood ajar, the moths that had gathered there seeped in, dancing like fairies around the kitchen light.

He walked out onto the back porch, glanced around at the length that spanned the back of the house. She wasn't at the picnic table or in the hot tub, not sitting in the rocking chair or lingering by the railing.

She was nowhere to be seen.

He hurried to the side of the porch that overlooked the driveway and let out a sigh of relief when he saw the Trailblazer still parked there. But if she hadn't taken the car, where was she?

"Veronica?" he called, a little louder this time.

A rustle in the nearby bushes made him jump. It was just below the porch, which hung partially over a cliff. His heartbeat jumped.

Did she fall?

"Hon? Are you ok? Veronica!" He scrambled over the side of the railing, desperate to come to her rescue, ears painfully tuned into the noises that indicated fast movement below the deck.

That was when he heard the growl.

James froze.

He was straddling the railing precariously and almost lost his footing in panic. The growl intensified. James felt the skin on the back of his neck prickle. He leaned back toward the porch, quietly pulled his leg back over the railing, landed with two feet as gently as he could.

"James?" Veronica's voice came from inside the house.

"Where were you?" he demanded, still stuck in the grip of alarm. He pushed through the back door, sending the moths up into the night, slamming the door after them.

"I-I.." she stammered, then sighed. "I was getting something from the car."

She covertly tucked the lighter into her back pocket. It would make things so much worse if he knew she'd snuck out for a smoke.

"I think there's a bear out there," he said, motioning to the back porch.

"Really?" She said, moving to the windows to see. "On the porch?"

"No, beneath it. I thought it was you. I—I didn't know what to think when I came downstairs and you weren't here."

Veronica stared at him, not sure what he wanted her to say. She shrugged. "Sorry."

"Look, just come to bed, will you?" He climbed up the stairs and sank back into bed.

"Yeah, fine." Veronica's words were lost on the first floor, so she poured herself another glass.

*

In her dreams, Veronica was back in Cades Cove. She ran through the pasture, grass tickling her naked legs. The sun played hide-and-seek with stark white clouds against a cornflower sky. Dandelion fuzz floated in the air, a hundred wishes she'd blown since childhood, leading her down the path towards home. The cabin stood in the distance in the shade of a sugar maple tree, smoke rising from its chimney. The feeling of family filled her, a deep connection that rested in her bones.

Then she heard his voice. James called to her—pulled her back toward the park gate—away from the rich valley of dreams.

But she didn't want to wake.

*

Saturday

Early morning light peered over the tops of the Smokies, and Veronica found herself on the back porch of the cabin. She had fallen asleep in the rocking chair, an empty wine glass still on her lap. She wondered if she could sneak upstairs without waking James but decided not to try. She would be damned if he kept telling her what to do.

"I think we should leave early." There, James had said it. It had been gurgling at the back of his throat all morning.

"That's crazy," said Veronica, her dark eyes traveling to the syrup and she motioned for him to pass it. "You're overreacting."

James handed her the bottle, watched as she drenched her pancakes even more. The amber liquid spread across the spongy round tower, pooled around the mounds of dough. Her appetite had grown since they'd been on vacation.

Could she be pregnant? He hoped so.

"You've been acting different since we've been here," said James.

"I haven't been sleeping well," she replied, taking a bite of pancake.

"I don't like it."

Her gaze snapped up to his in a warning. There was a fire there he'd never seen before—animalistic. Her jaw clenched, relaxed, and she took a breath as if she was holding her temper.

"What is that supposed to mean?" she said.

He wasn't looking for another fight. It was the last thing they needed at this point. "Look, all I'm saying is that I think this lack of sleep is affecting you... being tired doesn't flatter you."

She cocked an eyebrow, grabbed her plate and fork.

"Yeah, well, being a snob doesn't flatter you either."

With that, she turned and walked out onto the porch, where she'd eat alone.

*

Later that day, after he had given Veronica some time to cool off, James approached her with a peace offering. She sat on the back porch, writing in her journal. As he approached, she closed it, held it protectively against her chest. He held out the brochure.

"Gatlinburg," she read aloud.

"I propose this is what we do today. No more wilderness. Let's go explore the village like tourists."

His voice grew more excited as he talked.

"There's a sky-lift that can take us up to the top of one of the mountains. And there are distilleries with moonshine. And tons of little shops and restaurants."

Her face relaxed into the idea as she glanced at the pictures.

"What do you say?" he asked. "Friends?"

She smiled, feeling silly for holding a grudge.

"Friends."

They shook on it.

*

"Don't you think that skirt's a bit short?"

Veronica clenched her teeth. His comments weren't new, but she was seeing them in a whole new light. Maybe it was in the mountain air—a southern woman's fiery spirit come to rescue her from the compliant shell she'd worn through young adulthood.

"You didn't have a problem with the length of my skirt when we met."

James' mouth hung open in surprise. He held up his hands in surrender.

"Never mind."

They snaked down the mountains slowly, downshifting carefully. James thought about the night they had driven to find the cabin in the dark. The landscape was so different in the day. Some places were more treacherous than he'd thought, while others merely cast dramatic shadows at night.

He was realizing that the mountains could play tricks on you—in lots of ways.

*

Veronica felt like she was sinking into layers of the underworld as they descended the mountain. When they pulled into the town of Gatlinburg, it was as if they crossed the Atlantic into a European village. Quaint shops were nestled beside one another with winding brick paths and archways in between. They were greeted by Tudor buildings with decorative glass panes and a central fountain filled with wishes to be fulfilled.

Taken by the charming place, the couple settled into smiles. They walked hand in hand among other happy tourists, checking out knick-knacks, woven blankets, homemade candles, and beautifully painted tributes to the landscape. They stopped for ice cream and shared a bench by the fountain, listening to the water fall like rain, rhythmic and lulling. James found himself fantasizing about future family vacations they'd take, while Veronica considered never leaving.

They stood together before the fountain, sharing a kiss and tasting the remnants of sugary cream that lingered. James' lips were chocolate crunch and Veronica's were vanilla swirl.

He handed her a quarter and held one for himself.

"Make a wish," he said.

They closed their eyes, tossing in their coins. The silver glinted in the sunlight, bright against a copper background of pennies.

"Why quarters?" asked Veronica, as she noticed the difference.

"They're worth more," he answered, shrugging his shoulders.

She couldn't peg why, but it bothered her. Like her wish wouldn't have been good enough as a penny. When James excused himself to the restroom, she stood before the fountain alone, taking in the brilliant copper scene beneath the watery surface. She thought of the moths that had mesmerized her on the first night, how they clung to the window, trying to get to the light inside. What was it they were seeking? It's heat? It's brilliance? Did they think it was the source of all things?

They didn't realize the light was a lie.

She glanced around, made sure James was still out of sight, then plunged her arm into the fountain to retrieve her quarter. She wasn't sure it was hers and she didn't care—it was the symbolism that mattered. Her hand grasped an object—solid and silver—a wish she took back. Then she replaced it with a bright, copper penny. The one cent meant more to her than all the desires she'd ever had.

It was a bid for freedom.

When James returned, they continued down the street to the distilleries, where he drank and she turned over the secret that lay in her pocket.

*

The kind of dark that filled the bedroom that night was endless. As James woke, he was filled with unease. He fought to focus on something—anything—and suppressed the primal panic that gripped his heart. The memory of where he was came rushing back—the cabin, the mountains.

"Veronica?" His voice was loud in the nothingness.

He crawled off the bed, toward the window. He brushed up against the thick curtains and pulled them back. Moonlight filtered through the forest ceiling, leaked in through the window, and bathed the room in a dim glow. The bed was a sea of blankets, the dresser a dark looming shape in the corner.

Silence filled the cabin, and then was broken.

A scratching noise crept from the first floor, up the wooden stairs with the storybook railing, across the balcony that overlooked the living room. It crawled toward James like an invitation.

"Come hither," it begged.

Inside he shrank—the urge to hide filled him.

Danger was near.

He moved carefully to the door, reached for the light switch. He flicked it upward—nothing happened. He flicked it again—still nothing. Was the electricity out? Was it just the bulb in the bedroom?

The shiver of panic crawled up his back.

His breath quickened.

His heartbeat pounded.

He gulped.

His love was down there, though, so he must proceed.

"Veronica?" he said once again.

There was a rush of movement downstairs, a crash. Adrenaline ran through his system, his arms shook with the burst. All he could think to grab was the hiking stick propped next to the door. It was smooth in his hand, but not very strong.

Still, something was better than nothing.

The floorboards creaked under his feet as he emerged on the balcony, tried the light switch there. Nothing. Scenarios ran through his mind. Was this a home invasion? They cut the electricity and had Veronica down there. Maybe they had been followed, targeted. Someone thought they were stupid tourists—vulnerable.

And of all things, he wanted to curse the skirt she'd worn into town that day.

They wanted what was *his*.

His eyes were wide, taking in the darkness. The only light that crept in was funneled moonlight, playing with the shadows. He scanned the living room below—dark shapes were motionless.

He stepped down one stair. *Creak.*

Then another. *Creak.*

He gripped the stick with both hands, readying himself for a confrontation. He could hear nothing over the sound of his breath.

James turned the corner, peered into the kitchen, saw that the back door hung open on its hinges. Moonlight danced on the edge of the porch, a cool breeze stole in through the opening, rustling trees, muttering in a secret tone only nature could decipher.

It was then that the growling arose, low—guttural.

Behind him.

In a burst of panic, he turned, braced himself for the shadow moving toward him. It knocked him to the floor face-down, stood over him like a hunter claiming its prey. Pain radiated from James' head as he struggled to breathe. Then the weight lifted, moved toward the open door with a *creak, creak*. James gasped and the creature turned sharply, its eyes reflecting the moon.

Teeth were bared, as it closed the space between them again.

Breath rattled in and out of James' panicked mouth. His body was frozen. The bear's face stopped inches away from his, its breath hot and wet. Saliva stretched from one row of teeth to the next, and then narrowed in a growl that shook the cabin. The bass notes rose to a baritone crescendo, then descended back into a murmur. And James could have sworn he heard a woman's gasp.

A paw reached back, then swung forward, hitting its mark. And everything in James' world went black.

*

Sunday

When he woke to a sun-filled kitchen, James found the back
door still open. He stumbled to the porch, where he found
large, muddy footprints that led over the railing and
disappeared into the forest. It wasn't until he made his way
back inside that he noticed Veronica's nightgown crumpled by
the threshold to the cabin.

Beside it was a bright, shiny quarter.

 This piece originally appeared in *Underwood Press,* 2019.

Marsh Girl

It was only a hole in the ground at first—the sole hint a house would emerge. A backhoe's claw had torn at rocks and soil and ice, disturbing their rest. The earth resisted. It didn't want to release sleeping things but gave way to foolish human persistence.

I imagine it's how all nightmares begin.

By removing those layers of earth they freed a hiding spirit, maybe one buried on purpose. It suggested the land was haunted, but it wasn't the plot itself—it was the pond beside it. Water runs deep, infecting the water table, seeping into nature in concentric circles, bringing with it the rings of hell.

I don't live there now, but the place still haunts my dreams— seeps in when I least expect it—like it's trying to draw me back into its web to feed. And there's a guilt I can never resolve, for I entrapped someone else to be set free.

*

The home went up quickly, as they do with modern construction. That idyllic space held all our dreams—they were laid into the foundation, nailed into the boards and planks that became levels. I once imagined the first floor would be filled with laughter and the smell of baked goods. We'd do most of our living there—cuddling on the couch, sharing meals, shouldering each other's burdens from long days at work. The second floor would hold the master bedroom and three smaller rooms were marked for future children. I wanted a boy and two girls; my husband wanted the opposite. We planned to love them regardless.

When the house was done, we built a fence to keep those fictional children safe, decided against a pool for the risk it might pose. The locks were adequate, with bolts on the front and back entryways and a safety on the sliding glass door off the kitchen. We invested in a state-of-the-art security system with extra smoke detectors and a carbon monoxide indicator in the basement. We thought of threats long before they were a reality. But we only considered tangible solutions—locks, alarms, cupboard latches, child-proof lids. It wasn't until our first-born came home from the hospital that another threat showed its face.

*

I woke from the dream with a start. A dark shadow hung in the corner of the bedroom. Its edges reached out, receded, like it was breathing.

I froze, peeking out from the covers like a five-year-old. I shook my head straight, rationalized my fear. The bedside light banished it back into another realm, revealing a blank canvas—two walls meeting a ceiling. Just a converging place for cobwebs.

But the shivers ran over my body, sweat chasing them.

Lily was sleeping soundly in her crib, but I had to check. Not once, but twice. The first time I peeked in and saw the shadows playing on her face. By the time I got back into bed, I'd turned them into demons.

I crept again across the floor and into the hall, turned on the light to frighten them back into their corners, then lamented my anxiety because it woke her. Her cry began as a whisper, edged into a fuss, then a crescendo wail.

It was the sound of my fears—sharp and lingering.

*

The nightmares were more consistent when she turned one month old. Her little spirit strengthened; I could see it through her eyes, just as mine waned. I became withdrawn, ate less, even as she took my milk and stole my sleep.

It's what mothers do. I knew this—it's what I had wanted— and yet there didn't seem to be enough to fill her up. She was always taking, draining me.

I couldn't see it then, but it wasn't her.

It was someone else.

*

She came to me at night, her song like a whisper I couldn't catch. She slunk in through the cracked window, hid beneath my bed, waited for me to fall asleep. I'd wake to find her standing beside me, her gown marred with soil, her bonnet casting grey on her face. She'd reach for my hand and wouldn't be denied.

This friend was someone I'd wished for all my life. A gentle soul to guide me, so I'd never know loneliness. We'd walk together, sometimes in the kitchen, sometimes on the deck, always in the moonlight. It drew her in shades of blue, like smoke rising out of a fire. She was wispy, floated beside me, a hidden facet of my inner self.

A crazy mother without a child.

It was almost too late when I realized she wanted mine.

*

I thought of her as the Marsh Girl, though she was a secret I had no one to tell. Mark would have thought me insane. I'd long ago cast off the girlfriends I might confide in; they were all off mothering. Some nurtured children, others their husbands, and still more their employees, pets, and gardens.

Friendship was but a memory.

On the nights she didn't come, I'd imagine her floating above the marsh like fog. She'd settle in above the cattails, lull the coyotes to sleep with her sweet tune. She'd guard the creatures like a fierce angel, a warrior born of nature with arrows tucked beneath her gown. At dawn she'd sink into the earth, become one with the surface, tuck in to sleep beneath the roots of an oak. There she'd wait until darkness came again.

I longed for her in her absence, wondered why she'd abandoned me. She was my only companion, a wilder aspect of my own spirit, free to explore outside the confines of humanness. But I was trapped—inside a body, inside a house.

And I'd created this cage myself, a nightmare hidden in a dream.

It wasn't what I'd imagined at all, but I'd handed over the reins to fate.

*

Full moon was the Marsh Girl's favorite time. She seemed to draw her energy from it, neither waxing nor waning, but in full form. She was a dark silhouette against its light, her eyes pools of stars that ever expanded. I was a skeleton, my bones jutting out from a gaunt face.

We danced together, she as a lithe maiden, me as a ghost.

On the edges of the pond beside the house, we twirled and laughed. We spun this way and that, her fingers cold and refreshing, laced with mine. The earth was soft beneath my feet, sinking, embracing me. The water called to me, urging me home, to sleep in its sweet embrace.

There was nothing I wanted more.

"Claire!"

The shout roused me from my reverie. I looked about myself, feeling the cold in a new, jarring way. Snow covered the banks of the pond; all thoughts of a lush summer night receded into my mind. The ice-cold water stung my legs, at the bottom of which were my anchored feet, numb.

Mark was a shadow running at me, covering the distance between the pond and the house in a manner I'd never seen.

He slid to a stop before me, reaching out his hands. His face was contorted in the moonlight, a mixture of anger and terror, his eyes cutting me. The breath rose from his lips in desperate gasps but no words could escape.

It was then he yanked the baby from my arms.

*

The Marsh Girl didn't come to visit me in the hospital. The medication drained her power, put a barrier between us I couldn't tear down. But I could feel her waiting there, watching. She lurked on the other side of the veil, and I kept her secret.

A hole grew inside me that she once filled. In a bottomless well, I'd swim deeper and deeper, only to find layers of muck and grime. No water, no soft caress, no beating heart in time with my own. She was but smoke that slipped through my fingers, a wish that floated away with the wind.

*

Christmas came and went, and New Year's too. There were presents and songs, food and wine, and lots of visits from family. They looked at me sideways, trying to hide their discomfort. I gulped, said nothing, averted my gaze until I could hide behind a smile.

My energy came in short bursts—moments I'd reach out to connect with someone—but inevitably was disappointed. The conversation always returned to the same thing: How are you feeling, dear?

A carefully made-up face was armor I retreated beneath. During the day I lurked more and more in the recesses of my mind, allowing a lovely, pleasant, polite persona to speak. She was stupid, frivolous, and Mark loved her. He couldn't see me clawing from the inside, trying to get out.

It made me resent him more.

Lily knew, though. My baby always knew. I could see myself in her big blue eyes—a distorted reflection that fed her, held her, swaddled her like a machine. The days blended together—weekday, weekend, it didn't matter. Coffee in the morning, wine at night—like the nectar of the gods to keep me going.

I knew I shouldn't drink due to breastfeeding but lying to myself had become second nature. Lying was all I had left because if I was honest, the self-loathing would drown me. Each day was the same, riddled with layers of fabrication and dead dreams, and they sucked my soul with each passing moment.

I stopped taking the meds, but I didn't tell Mark.

He didn't deserve to know.

He had scared the angel away.

*

The Marsh Girl came back to me two nights later, at the next full moon. We slipped out the kitchen door at 3 a.m., crept across the deck and down the stairs. The snow crunched beneath my feet as I crossed the yard to the back corner—a place where the earth dipped and reached out to the swamp.

The cattails bobbed above the fence, leaning in, like hands grasping for me.

We built a fire there and huddled under the chenille throw, our breath mingling in the winter air. The cold tickled my face, but I was warm in her presence, the glow of the flames dancing across her lips, playing with her features. They morphed as she began to speak—one moment a child with curious eyes, the next a maiden with a come-hither glance, and then a mother with a swollen womb. As her belly grew before me, her eyes met mine and I froze.

Her story poured into me like an opening storm cloud.

*

She was roused from sleep by unkind hands. They wandered her body, then tore at her clothes. The pain was a violent intrusion, but a hand covered her mouth, stifled her screams.

She couldn't breathe.

He was crushing her.

When it was over, he fled, leaving her in her tarnished sheets, red with her own blood.

Her growing womb was an embarrassment to her and her family. She hid it underneath heavy skirts and ignored remarks from other young women about her plumpness. The Reverend told her mother it was a gift, but she felt damned, feral, like a cow about to give birth. Full of shame, she was ruined in the eyes of suitors.

When the baby came, she thought she'd be freed from a burden. But when her mother took the infant to the pond to drown it, part of her died, too.

What was a mother without her child?

The quiet was suffocating.

It wasn't long after that she'd followed into the cold slumber the water promised. And there her spirit lingered for days, for nights, forever, but her child was nowhere to be found.

*

I woke with my face against the snow, violent shrieks of a fire alarm piercing my ears. The smoke was thick around me, wafting in the cold winter wind. It burned my throat, suffocated my screams.

The deck was on fire.

I rushed toward the sliding glass doors, yelling for Mark. But all I could see was my own reflection, wrapped in the throw, embers rising into the air around me. I raised my arms to throw off the burning mantle, a phoenix in the glass.

And that's when I saw the Marsh Girl beside me—no longer the child, the maiden or mother.

She was a crone, not wise and guiding, but bent on revenge.

*

My hospital stay was quicker this time, just long enough to get me stabilized on meds—yet again. Mark took the baby and went to his mother's while I completed intensive outpatient therapy. I met with others "like me" who were struggling with postpartum psychosis, but in all the time I listened to them speak, none had seen the Marsh Girl.

Upon my return home, I found a war zone. The deck was a burnt remnant in the back of the house, with scorch marks and smoke staining the once pleasant beige siding. The Fire Department had doused the flames before there was structural damage, but the cosmetic harm scarred our lovely home.

For once, it looked the way I felt. There was something satisfying about this, but I tucked that knowledge away to savor in the shadows.

*

Whatever they put in those meds drove the Marsh Girl away.

Part of me was relieved—she was a reckless leech determined to drag me down with her. Revenge was so hot in her soul that she burned anyone who listened. Maybe that's what it was—she was scorching me from the inside out. And if she couldn't burn me, she'd drown me from the outside in.

She was a sliding rope I was holding too tight, but despite the sting, I didn't want to let go. She had chosen me, trusted me, shared her deepest darkest secrets. We were kindred spirits in some ways, both longing to fill emptiness inside. Yet in other ways, we were day and night; I had no interest in hurting someone else, but she wanted to scald the world.

I was in the nursery when the realization hit me—she needed to feed. I had been her victim, almost handed her Lily. My instinct for self-preservation was muted. Most of me wanted to leap onto the other side of the veil and sail with the Marsh Girl through the skies. But there was a spark of something else, too.

It was a thread at first, a memory of Lily's laughter, a light in her eyes. The thread became thicker the more I followed it until it flooded through my chest and burst out of my eyes in long trails of salty tears.

I grasped the thread and I didn't let go.

*

Planting trees as a barrier came to me in a dream, and when I woke I could think of nothing else. Willows to cleanse the earth, weeping tears the Marsh Girl could not shed. Their crooked branches might ensnare her, build a web of magic to lull her into their arms.

I would welcome new life onto the land, ask the willows to transform the soil. Mark joined me in this endeavor, though I didn't explain why. I simply asked for his help with a project, told him it was an assignment from group therapy—to do something constructive with him instead of destructive.

By the time we were done, six willows stood between our fence and the pond. Their roots would dig deep, drink the water, call her home. And if we were lucky, she'd sleep among them, cease this game of vying for my soul, for my child.

*

The Marsh Girl was absent for a long time. I'd like to say her memory faded over time, but she became a mythic creature to me—a symbol of my own weakness and the trials so many women have faced. I found myself looking for her out the window before bed, wondering if she'd return—both never wanting to see her again and longing for nothing more.

Just before we moved, I owed her one final visit, even if I didn't invite her back into my home, into my head. I could have stopped taking the meds, dropped the barrier between us, but I knew I wouldn't make it back again if I slipped to the other side. So, I waited until Mark and Lily were asleep on that final night. Beneath the light of the full moon, I crept out into the back yard, through the fence, and to the surface of the pond. My reflection stared back at me, with fuller cheeks, livelier eyes. The air rushed around me, tousled my hair like a mother to a child. The spring breeze carried with it a hint of singe, or perhaps it was just my imagination.

Maybe it was her way of waving from beneath the veil.

The broken glass was sharp against my finger, the pain potent. Blood gathered into a pool on the surface, until it spilled over, fell into the water. It was my offering to her, a homage to her existence, a final goodbye.

As my essence sank beneath the surface, I saw a flicker of light there, the moon's face looking right at me.

A sigh, and then silence.

When I walked away from the pond that night, I left my shadow standing there.

*

It wasn't my intention to go back years later, but my mind took to wandering as I drove. When I realized where I was, the horror gripped my stomach, but there was a longing also. I didn't see the Marsh Girl, but I could smell her on the air— sweet like lavender, with a hint of singe. The hum of her lingered beneath the sunshine on the pond, rippling gently in the breeze. The willows were taller than I'd imagined they'd be, standing like beacons between the pond and the house.

It wasn't until a cloud passed over the sun, dropping a shadow over the property that I saw them walking. I remembered them as younger, the family who'd bought the house from us. The mother and child skimmed the perimeter of the pond, navigating the land bridge between it and the marsh beyond. She looked up, her cheekbones prominent, her eyes sunken in their sockets. She led the child too close to the pond's edge and I knew the Marsh Girl was waking.

But she wasn't hungry for me.

 This piece originally appeared in *Untoward Magazine,* vol. 3, no. 11, 2020.

Cicadas in the Suburbs

Mrs. Davis had the ability to freeze time. She could engage in any mundane task, like folding laundry or rinsing the dinner dishes, and in a moment the present suspended to make room for the past. Memories from the last thirty-five years lived again, spread out like rich canvases splashed with color and texture.

On Sunday morning, it interrupted the task of sandwich-making. As she dragged the knife along the spongy white bread, and the peanut butter was smoothed into a caramel blanket, Mrs. Davis found herself in reverie.

She stood in a room, looking up at marketing images that spanned the wall like a bulletin board. A woman blowing dust from her hand that turned into dancing images further down the page. A powerful black swoosh that enigmatically stretched against stark white paper, creating images that may or not be there, like a Rorschach ink blot. A dress made of butterfly wings, draped in a window, daring little girls to become ballerinas. An impassioned woman with bright red lipstick and hair pulled back to the nape of her neck, peeking out from behind the lip of a salsa costume as she dressed for the stage.

But which of these images captured the idea of dance performance best? As Marketing Director, it was her job to choose. The power to create a vision for the public was intoxicating; she could imagine nothing more fulfilling, except perhaps gracing the stage herself.

"Mommy, that doesn't look like a sandwich."

The small voice pulled Mrs. Davis back into the present, where she found a counter smeared with peanut butter and the remnants of a very sorry piece of bread.

It happened again, but this time she was walking the dog. They trotted along their usual route, down one side of the cul-de-sac to the other, beneath colorful autumn trees that threatened to lose their leaves. Most still clung to their mothers, fearful to make the death dance to the ground, but the smell in the air told them it was about time. As they were in the final stretch home, Sam the golden retriever led his human off the normal path to the adjacent cemetery.

While some might think it strange that anyone would want to live so close to a graveyard, Mrs. Davis had always found it to be pleasantly quiet and somehow comforting. She didn't go out of her way to stroll among the plots, but when she did find herself there, she walked respectfully. Sam was not so careful as he pulled her along, deeper into the cemetery.

Mrs. Davis sipped her pumpkin spice latte and she savored the warm liquid as it spilled into her mouth and down her throat. A smile met her lips for just a moment, as she examined the lipstick ring that was left on the cover of the coffee cup, and she was pulled back into her memories once again.

The wine glasses were lined up next to each other on the counter, each marked by a different shade of color. Hers was unapologetically bright red—a stain that portrayed confidence and spunk. Mattie's thin mark was warm pink with sparkles, just like her personality. Eva's was bold and voluptuous, burnt orange with a "come hither" faded outline. And Megan's was somewhat in between in size, but very faint in hue, for she was a ChapStick girl and only tread into the world of gloss for special occasions.

Laughter filled the air as they compared the residue of kisses that might be spent in regret or in life-long promises. A glass of wine among twenty-something friends was always the time for sharing secrets, hopes, and dreams. It was her safe space and they were her retreat when the burdens of the world became too heavy.

Mrs. Davis was yanked out of her trance by a barking Sam and the cold sensation of wetness on her feet. She looked down to find herself on the edge of a pond in the middle of the cemetery. Startled, she backed up but lost her balance on the sloping edge. What was wrong with her?

She sat for a moment, looking up at the large weeping willow that hung over the water gracefully, its leaves almost touching the surface. She thought she saw the outline of a cicada's exoskeleton there, hanging on for dear life, but could not be sure. Shaking her head as if clearing the fog, the woman held back tears. Most of the time, Mrs. Davis liked that she could freeze time, but lately it had been less of a choice and more a loss of control.

Time, it seemed, was manipulating her.

As Sam and Mrs. Davis made their way home, she was frightfully aware of the fact that the bottoms of her khakis were wet and her soft pink sweater-set was marred with dirt from her fall. She walked quickly, hoping to avoid prying neighbors. Despite her stealth, the street was buzzing with activity, prepping houses for Halloween. But she noticed something as she returned friendly waves and ignored quizzical glances tossed in her direction.

While the husbands and children seemed engrossed in the yard activities, many of the wives were not so. They stood in the background, taking pictures and prepping snacks, on the periphery of joy. It would not be fair to say that Mrs. Davis accurately noticed this about all the wives, but she thought she did, and in some cases, she was right. Some noticed her, too, not because of the disheveled state of her outfit, but because of a camaraderie of sorts.

Perhaps only those on the fringe notice when others linger there.

At 2011 Sunshine Lane, Mrs. Johnson watched as her sons played basketball, dribbling, shooting, scoring. A smile was pasted on her face but did not quite touch the corners of her eyes. Had she trained herself to avoid wrinkles or was she acting the part? She had become an observer even in her own life—a cheerleader only for others.

Next door at 2013, Mrs. Williams sat beside her husband on the porch swing, listening intently (or appearing to) as he explained his upcoming work week. She was a passenger on the ride, at his mercy to steer her in one direction or the other. She gazed off to the side, her thoughts probably wandering into territory that just belonged to her, but her husband did not notice.

And across the street at 2018, Mrs. Jones stood on her porch, watching everyone else busy at work, having no one to look after because her girls were back at college. As her eyes locked with those of Mrs. Davis, they seemed to narrow, the crow's feet sticking out like crooked tree branches. The pearls around her neck wound around aging skin like a tightening rope, and for just a moment, Mrs. Davis thought she saw them morph into skeletal hands.

As her eyes drifted around the neighborhood, the wives appeared in various stages of irrelevance. She imagined them like cicadas seeking freedom, trying to crawl out of their former shells. Perhaps it had not been a good day to add rye whiskey to her pumpkin spice latte.

*

Later that week, Mrs. Davis sat quietly in the kitchen with her laptop. Dinner had been eaten, her kids were tucked into bed, and her husband rested in the living room with Sam, watching the news. With a glass of chardonnay in her hand, she clicked through websites of online colleges she had seen on TV that promised a path to reinvention. Could she find a new career at thirty-five?

Once she had been on top of her game; marketing came like second nature to her. But this was a new world filled with Facebook posts, Twitter feeds, and Snapchat filters (if she was honest, she did not even know what a "tweet" was). Even if she wanted to go back to work, the landscape had changed, and she was no longer relevant.

It was then that she first heard the whisper.

It started like a hum that might be wind through the trees or might not be. It was someone trying to breathe, but the exhale continued for far too long to be human.

It paused… began to hum again.

Mrs. Davis stood from her perch at the counter and moved toward the window, which was slightly ajar. The night was charcoal outside, lit only by the distant lamps on the street, all the way on the other side of the house.

Were her ears playing tricks on her?

But then she heard it again: "Ashhhhhhhh….."

Mrs. Davis froze. The whisper dissipated into a secret, hushing the startled yelp that nearly escaped from her throat. Was there someone standing outside her window? She thought to call her husband, but her throat would not cooperate. Glancing over her shoulder, she saw the light flickering from the TV. He was probably asleep by now.

"Ashhhhhh!" came the whisper, more eager now, stabbing through the air to find her ears.

She jumped back, the proximity of the voice alarming. With a burst of adrenaline, Mrs. Davis flicked on the light switch, flooding the backyard patio with light. But there was nothing to be found but wind-swept leaves that decorated the well-kept lawn. With a hard shove, she closed the window then drew the blinds, feeling comfortable again only when no prying eyes could invade her warm, safe kitchen.

As she sat back down at the computer and continued looking for her future on the myriad of websites that urged her to "chat now," Mrs. Davis melted into the despair that grew in her heart. With every sip of chardonnay, she gulped down the dreams she once had of traveling the world, the freedom she felt at twenty-five that was nothing more than a recollection now. She loved her family—of course she did—but there had to be more than dancing on periphery of joy.

She could not shake the feeling that time was running out.

The hush in the air drew her out to the stage, quietly, nymph-like. There she lingered in a graceful pose until the light woke her and the music floated closer, enveloping her body. It coaxed her into the soft ebbs and flows of rhythm, from her fingertips down her arms, through her torso and to her legs, which carried her across the stage and back again. Hundreds of eyes fed her passion, and she danced for them—with them—leaping and turning, until they were dizzy and moved to tears. As she settled back into a cocoon pose and the music receded into a soft lull, their applause filled her with hope.

*

Mrs. Davis woke with a jolt as her head slid from the keyboard onto the counter with a soft thud. The lights in the kitchen were on, the blinds were still drawn, and the TV glow shone from the living room. Had she fallen asleep?

The clock on the microwave indicated 3:02 a.m., and the empty bottle of wine rested beside her, tauntingly. Embarrassed, even though no one was looking, Mrs. Davis stretched and planned to tiptoe across the kitchen floor. But when she looked down, she was horrified to discover that her feet were caked with mud. A set of dirty footprints led to the back door, which hung open in the cool autumn night.

Through tear-filled eyes, Mrs. Davis cleaned up the evidence and crept up to bed without so much as waking her husband.

She was going to have to stop drinking like this.

A week passed by. Halloween came and went without incident. The kids wore their costumes, joined the procession through the neighborhood, and yielded bags of candy that would have them on sugar highs for the next month. Most of the leaves had abandoned their trees and lay crunchy and decaying on the ground. Talk of the Thanksgiving holiday had begun, with recipes for homemade cranberry sauce and pumpkin pie being traded among neighbors. But Mrs. Davis always marked this time of year by pulling out the winter coats and exchanging the candy-rimmed "Trick or Treat" wreath on the door for the one decorated in "Natural Harvest." Maintaining her environment helped her achieve a particular sense of control.

The first snow came earlier than usual, bringing with it a chill that Mrs. Davis could not quite shake. She had told herself firmly that there would be no more time-freezing and no more drinking. She was too old for these games. After all, she was a mother, had a mortgage on a lovely suburban home, and drove a minivan; the days of adventure and fantasy would be left in the past, where they belonged.

But sometimes the past does not listen… sometimes it has a mind of its own.

*

It was late one night that Mrs. Davis awoke to the sound of whispers.

"Ashhhhhhhh…." they hummed. But this time, they did not scare her. They lulled her, like a string quartet pulling her onto the stage, coaxing her to lift her head from the soft, warm pillow. She slipped out from underneath the covers, her husband not even stirring from sleep.

Placing her feet in everyday slippers, she envisioned ballet shoes, laced up her calves. Her nightgown was a delicate tutu and her robe the wings of a fairy. She glided down the hall, past the posed studio pictures that lined the walls, past the nightlight that glowed like a beacon, across the creaks in the floor that once would have woken sleeping babes.

"Ashhhhhhhh…." The whispers grew in strength, the voices increasing from a few to many.

Down the stairs she floated, like a diva entering an elaborate ballroom, graciously waving her arms and acknowledging her fans. The back door called to her like a portal—the gateway to a theater that awaited her presence. She paused quickly at the hallway mirror, not seeing the eye cream and curlers in her hair, but rather stage makeup and a glistening tiara.

This would be a performance to remember.

"Ashhhhhhhh!" No longer gentle, the whispers urged her forth.

Careful not to miss her cue, she floated to the door and crossed the threshold into the winter wonderland. The scene was just as she had imagined—a white sheen coated everything gently, and a soft blue hue hugged it like a mist in the full moon light.

The breath escaped her mouth softly, in an adagio of its own, as her voice joined the whispers: "Ashhhhhhhh...."

And she danced. *Chassé, chassé, chassé.*

She moved down the cul-de-sac street in the ballet move, leaving grooves in the dusting of snow. She stopped and assumed fourth position, then: *Grand jeté!* She leapt into the air gracefully, then landed and paused for dramatic effect. The applause was thunderous in her ears.

Chassé, chassé, chassé. She continued on, her slippers still somehow on her feet.

By the time she arrived at the pond, her skin was like ice, but she could not feel it. She was lost in a snow globe, a winter fairyland, a child's jewelry box that played *"Fur Elise"* and featured her alone. *Chassé, chassé, chassé.* She was at the edge of the water now. *Arabesque!*

As she lifted up her leg behind her into the pose she had learned as a child, and leaned forward, she could see her reflection in the watery surface. It was not cold enough to be frozen yet, though the edges of the water were beginning to crust. The face looking back at her sparkled with fairy dust and her wings were spread out behind her like translucent crystal. She was a blown glass figurine, a topper for her daughter's birthday cake with hair of spun sugar. The snow drifted around her like dandelion fuzz—a wish blown from the other side of the world, pushing her forward just a bit.

As she teetered toward the other face, she leaned into the kiss, becoming one with the self she had not seen in many years.

"Ashhhhhhhhley!" The chorus sang. "Ashley!"

Touching the surface, the exoskeleton released her, and brilliant wings inflated in its place. She had found herself. It was not time that had been chasing her, or even the past. It was the person she had left behind at the altar. The one who wanted to see faraway places and fulfill impossible dreams. She longed for the freedom to spread those wings—whether by gracing the stage herself or choosing images that empowered other little girls to do so. It was the music she had lost that now found her, the movement that had become so foreign that once had filled her.

She tumbled into the cold wetness, shattering the image of her old self and sending it in fragments to the edges. The ripple carried pieces of her away, making room for the parts she sought. Like broken china, she pulled the shards together one by one, on the other side of the surface, beneath the weight of a thousand teardrops.

She spun around and around in a *pirouette*, a smile on her face as she folded back into a finale – a *coda* for a *pas de deux*. For a moment, both sides of the reflection were one, and then there was only Ashley, for Mrs. Davis had become a ghost.

 This piece originally appeared in *GNU Journal,* Winter 2018.

Part Three: Crone

"This is a woman to be revered. She is a concentration
of feminine wisdom gathered...over the years,
blended with the astral knowledge of the soul-star,
and blessed by the traditions of the Sacred Feminine
that she has made herself, or resurrected from Time,
and passed living and intact to her daughters."

~ Elizabeth S. Eiler

Honey Tree

Tennessee, US.A.

Spring, 1984.

Liadan followed the forest trail before dawn, the last bits of
night tickling her arms, pulling the spring chill around her.
Breath rose from her lined mouth in a whisper, echoing the
shudders from the evening's tears. Her eyes were swollen,
vision blurry from sadness and too much wine. The taste was
still fresh upon her stained lips.

She stumbled on aging limbs, feet searching for moss and
grass but finding gnarled roots and pine needles. It had been
foolish to leave the cabin without shoes. But each stone
obstacle was a reminder of that last argument—the one that
broke her open and chased him out the door.

He was gone, now but a recollection, like the smell of rain-
soaked earth after a storm. Who was she without him? She
sifted through long memory, a twisted thicket of knotted
hopes and stifled anger, a forest of discarded dreams. She
lingered on the children, colorful butterflies stretching their
wings in her mind. A smile tickled the edges of her mouth,
then turned down in grief as she recalled their empty beds and
trinkets of childhood that remained behind.

They were now mere shadows of the past.

And she was haunted.

Liadan swallowed her grief, choking on it. Her chest ached. She was a broken heart, a stumbling tear searching for sunshine in the dark. But all that showed its face was the moon, its rays filtered through whispering leaf buds.

The ground became softer as she neared the spot, the one from the wise woman's stories in Gatlinburg. A honey tree, she'd called it – a sacred place where bees went to commune and spin women's secrets into nectar.

Tell the bees your woes. But take care, she'd warned. If the queen deems you unworthy, you will feel her wrath—a thousand stings.

Liadan cared not, for she had nothing more to lose. Dare she think it? Death by nature was seductive to a wailing banshee.

When she came upon the tree, a hush fell around her. The wind, which had spoken the whole journey, was silenced. Blossoms brushed the tips of the crabapple's limbs, her canopy a perfumed umbrella. It was magic in the moonlight, shifting from silver to pink as clouds moved across the sky. Mushrooms graced the space below it, a circular veil luring her forth.

And so, she stepped into the fairy ring, seeking the space between the worlds. And she remembered. She told the bees, beyond sight but lingering somewhere.

*

Images of childhood swam toward her, prickly and dark swirling with laughter and joy. There was tenderness and beauty, but also fear and silence.

She chanted adages, once from outside of her, now lurking within.

Be polite. Ladylike. Demure. Quiet.

On a backdrop of tea parties and summer splashes beneath a lilac tree there were moments that stung—pins and needles of memory so potent they stole her breath. Father yelling, mother crying, glares that woke shame in the deepest parts of her.

You don't belong. Fat. Stupid. Weird.

She was an adolescent now, gangly and awkward, a tangle of emotions—up, down, sideways, and inside out. The desire to connect strong like sweet tarts and banana splits in July. Her voice was a gift that brought her pride and attention. She could sing like no other, but spoken words got twisted in her mouth. Music was a safe place, where voices could intertwine, and everyone belonged.

Beautiful. Strong. Talented. Capable.

Teenage years rushed at her. She thrived, finally growing into her body, inhabiting something lovely. Always there was a hum, from operatic arias to folky guitar. She swayed with spotlights and shadow, her body waking with grace and first kisses. She found her place among composers, choreographers, storytellers, where spirit preached through voice and movement.

And then she met him.

Stupidest smart person I know. Those jeans are too tight. Who do you think you are? You can't write. That color makes you look fat. You're not a singer anymore. Eat the damn steak and stop complaining.

Just shut up.

All she wanted was to be loved, and so she did.

She shut up.

Seduction followed by a slap of words. A waltz with the prince turned devil. His childhood pain consumed him, twisted his curiosity into bitterness, his kindness into cruelty. She became his caged bird, enclosed in lies. Song became tears, and tears became muted screams.

Until he told their children to shut up, too.

The lump in Liadan's throat was thick and raw, a mass that had been growing for twenty years. Her stomach curdled as she sat with this wound, turning it over, examining the ugly grooves. Waves of nausea swelled, woke the overindulgence from earlier—a mix of merlot and cheese and bread that swirled until it was purged.

She gave it back to the soil, retching until there was nothing left to offer. Then she curled into a ball and cried, grieving for the voice she had lost—the one she chose to silence.

*

When Liadan woke, she was face-down on a mossy bed, the smell of dirt thick in her nose. Her chest was pressed to the earth, as if only the great mother could heal the hole inside. Daggers of regret and fear that had been lodged there as of late relaxed into pinpricks and then hardened into scabs.

She breathed and her heartbeat was one with everything.

She rolled over, blinking in the sunlight that peaked through graceful, weeping limbs. Pink blossoms above seemed to move despite the air's stillness, bursts of color that danced between dreams. Leaves were still buds but would grow into teardrops with fine teeth. Wild apples would grow, bulbous dark red, tart and hard. Ancestor of all orchards, and gift to the bees.

The droning was a secret, lost in the breeze that had woken from slumber. But as the air relaxed and stillness settled in, Liadan could hear it. The hive spoke, a low rumble of choreographed wings fluttering in chorus, a chant to the great mother. Their collective voice was a bard, a seanchaí, telling the stories of the women who had come before.

The tree was humming.

With widened eyes, she watched as hundreds of honeybees went about their work, floating from blossom to blossom, gathering pollen as they went. Lulled by the soft vibration, Liadan rose, slowly, carefully. Her face drew closer to the insects, and their voice became louder. The curved canopy drew the sound down, surrounding her in a heartbeat, a drum.

And she danced.

Arms to the side, she swayed. Face to the sky, she parted her lips and sang. Soprano notes, light and airy, blended with their tenor roar. She was with them, beside them, engulfed in their sweet essence.

Images swam of women in tears. Cracked and bleeding. Hiding and seeking. All drawn to this place of secrets and hopes and renewed dreams. The bees knew. They sang the women back to life.

Eyes closed, she focused on the collective mind above, asking—begging for guidance. Perhaps she would not be killed, for what would a queen want with a broken woman?

The voice came to her, first in a squeal, then a hush.

Surrender, it said. Release the layers of mother and wife, of daughter and sister, and make room for wisdom. Welcome the gray and go within. For that is where the honey lies.

And then all was silent.

When Liadan opened her eyes, she was alone. The bees had disappeared, and the blossoms were still. But the hum—the hum remained inside her head, inside her heart. It beat within, a droning of hope.

And as she examined the graceful branches, she noticed the charms attached. They had been hidden among the blossoms until now. At first it was one, then two, but the more she studied the tree, she saw them everywhere. An earring here, a necklace there, a feather, a dried rose, a piece of red cloth.

And so many more wishes left to the hive. Discarded offerings that spoke volumes with no sound. The honeybees had been doing their work for a long time. They passed on their wisdom with the seasons, an unending chain of festooning creatures. A comb of insight and hope.

As the sun rose higher in the sky, Liadan relaxed back to the ground. On her knees, she faced the tree, its bark covered in green lichen. Where the hive was now, she did not know. Perhaps this tree was their threshold, their window between the worlds, safe inside of the fairy ring. She was indebted to their magic but had brought nothing to offer. Not even a pencil to write a poem. So, she pulled out several long, graying hairs, one by one.

One for her marriage.

Two for her children.

Three for friendships abandoned.

Four for her parents and siblings.

And five more for the dreams she had left behind.

She separated the fifteen threads into thirds and braided them with careful fingers. She moved into deep contemplation as she wove, knowing this gift was more than an offering. It was a release of the burdens that had strangled her, morphed her into unwanted things.

Liadan hung the braid on one of the lower branches, twisting it around and around. It was a snake coiling back on itself, a piece of her she gave back to the earth. It slipped away, among the branches of the tree, soaked into its soft embrace. She was one of them now—a voice in a chorus of women who had sought refuge here, among the blossoms.

She lingered for a moment, imagined the queen somewhere in the ether, singing to her children. Mother of all, keeper of honeybee vision. Seeing more than color, more than the here and now. Liadan closed her eyes and bowed her head. Her life stretched out before her, past and future converging into a beautiful story that begged for telling.

Thank you, she whispered, stepping out of the fairy ring, back to the other side.

Her silenced voice had merely been sleeping. It hummed in the dark now, starting to wake. And it dripped sweet gold.

*

"Liadan's Song for the Bees"

Walk with me, sisters,
Deep into the forest
Where bees awaken
Your soul from rest,
Spinning waxen chains
And combs so sweet
To hold you when
You cannot see.
Dance with us, sisters,
And find your way
Between the blossoms,
Amongst the fae.
Sing your woes
To the winged ones
And leave your worries

On a braided tongue.
Peel layered archetypes
And reborn you will be
Only then will you find
The honey tree.

 This piece originally appeared in *Ethnosphere Magazine*, 2024.

Crow Woman

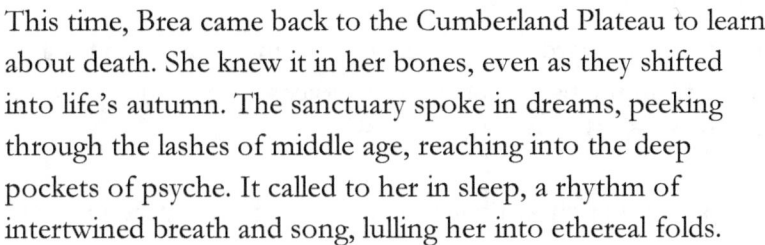

This time, Brea came back to the Cumberland Plateau to learn about death. She knew it in her bones, even as they shifted into life's autumn. The sanctuary spoke in dreams, peeking through the lashes of middle age, reaching into the deep pockets of psyche. It called to her in sleep, a rhythm of intertwined breath and song, lulling her into ethereal folds.

Setting foot onto the property after all that time was surreal. When some might see dull gray skies and the threat of winter, Brea saw only beauty.

But it was not beauty without sorrow.

She and her husband had walked there for many years. Fingers laced, lost in conversation, comfortable in silence. He was her warm blanket, her glass of cabernet, her happy place when she lost hope. They shared the retreat and its gifts with their family. Children and grandchildren visited the getaway, filling the acreage with laughter and song.

And then he had passed, journeyed into the unknown without her.

Now it was just her and their dog, Leo.

Echoes of *him* were everywhere—in the floorboards, in the trees, in the soil. He'd built the back courtyard with blood and sweat and planted the grapevines so she could make her own wine. In the summer, rows of lavender, milkweed, and yarrow stretched out past the barn, toward the soft rolling hills. And further back sat the woods, with hundred-year-old trees towering over saplings. The fairy woods, they had dubbed them, spinning myths and ghost stories for campfire s'mores.

If she listened hard enough, she could almost hear him calling to her from the barn. But then the voice was gone, lost to time and memory.

The pain in her chest flowered into a sharp pinch, then relaxed in a dull ache that demanded pause. She breathed in and out as it made its way through her body. She imagined it escaping through her mouth, a demon expelled in fall's chilled air.

She opened the front door to the cabin, the smell of dust and time welcoming her. It was just as they had left it, plaid blankets folded on the ends of the couch, wood stacked by the fireplace, and clean dishes in the rack next to the sink. The cozy two-bedroom was a welcome change from the large house up north.

The dark kitchen was a warm hug—a place for hibernation. They had planned to lift its face, transforming it into something from HGTV. But they had never gotten to it. Now, she never would. She opened the lid to the candle that sat on the stovetop, notes of apple rising into the air, bringing with them his laughter.

His face.

His kiss.

Brea exhaled her sorrow. Her eyes went to the window above the sink, where she spotted the pair of cardinals. One bright scarlet, the other dull rust. She opened the back door of the modest dwelling, spooking the birds from their perches.

She would have to lure them back.

With a bucket of seed in hand, she walked through the back courtyard, an encapsulated garden he had built for her four-legged friends and the winged ones. She filled the feeder, hung a cake of suet, then plugged in and filled the heated bird bath as the dog sniffed the ground. The yellow lab followed a scent across fallen leaves, crunching them beneath large paws.

"Good boy, Leo," she said, as he came to sit beside her, leaning in as she stroked his head. They stayed there for some time, sniffing the air, a mix of chilling earth, decaying leaves, and a hint of distant burning firewood. The statuesque pair watched the branches of the dogwood dance, their half-naked, twisted arms bobbing in time to windchimes.

Birds returned one by one, Brea and Leo frozen, blending into the garden. They came in waves—first the nuthatches, sparrows, and tufted titmice. They fed on sunflower seeds and songbird mix. Then the cardinals and blue jays followed, with mourning doves strutting on the ground to catch what fell. Woodpeckers and red-winged blackbirds pecked at suet then played in the heated bath, cleaning their plumage and drinking in the warmth. They had left feathers over the years as gifts, which Brea collected and placed upon the windowsill that overlooked the garden.

She had much to learn from the winged ones, for they knew the sky. And someday, when her body returned to the Mother, her spirit would fly with them.

And she would hold him again.

The air shifted, and the birds fled. Brea examined the sky to find the source of upset. A hawk sat in the pine toward the back of the property, where the hills became woods. His noble silhouette, barely visible among the branches, was a sentry.

He was hunting.

Brea swallowed her knowing. She was a steward for this land and all its creatures. She did not want to think of her birds caught in the hawk's talons. Defeathered and torn apart by its beak. And yet, the predator was a winged one, too. A bird of prey and a messenger.

The hawk alighted from his perch, stretching wings out and riding the current above. Brea wondered if it was *him*, watching her from the other side, protecting her, as he always had. She may be a widow, but she was still a wife. For now, she had to love him from far away.

Just for a little while.

Leo nudged her hand, his cold nose drawing her back down to earth.

"Alright, little man," she said, leading him back inside. He trotted to his bed, warm by the fireplace, circled once, and lay down.

As the door was almost closed, Brea heard it.

The mew was so faint, it was a ghost in the air. She held her breath. Listened. And there it was again.

The light was fading, taking the day's only warmth with it. She could not leave the creature to freeze. So, she pulled the knit hat down over her ears, and sank her hands back into gloves, then started out across the property, seeking the animal in need.

Wind swirled around her, tugging at the tendrils of graying hair that escaped from her hat. Gusts lifted leaves into a whirling funnel of oak, maple, and elm. Night was descending, lulling day creatures to sleep and begging others to wake.

The mewing slipped beneath the wind's howl, and Brea wondered if the land was playing tricks. But as she reached the mouth of the wood, the cries became louder, high-pitched and hungry.

A hush fell as the wind dissipated, making room for her to hear. Brea crunched through leaves, following the pitiful cries. A gray haze settled in among the trees as they groaned to each other in a foreign language. She was in another world now, a guest in the wild.

She pulled the flashlight out from her pocket. The beam cut through thick woods, tossing shadows, until it found two reflections. The kitten was a tumble of long gray fur, its eyes pale and large. It did not run or even shrink.

Maybe four weeks old. Where is Mama?

"Hi, little one," she whispered, looking around, searching for more signs of life. All was still as the haze grew thicker, colder.

She thought of the hawk and gulped.

Brea crouched down, gently scooped the crying thing into her gloved hands, tucked it gently into the folds of her jacket. It fell silent, nestling into her warmth.

She walked back toward the house with the flashlight beam guiding her way. The kitten's soft purring was a rumble in her chest, waking a sense of mothering she had not felt in some time. It was a gift to protect one so vulnerable, so young.

The crunch of autumn under her boots seemed louder than it had before sunset. Any moment now, she would see the faint glow from the cabin in the distance, guiding her home. But she kept walking and the darkness clung to her.

Have I gotten turned around?

The woods breathed, the mist growing thicker, swallowing the beam from her light. The air glowed in a halo. A spotlight on her for those with night vision.

Panic began to tuck in beside the kitten, a sharp pinprick in her chest.

"Sh, sh," she said. "It's okay. I've got you."

But the kitten was sleeping. It was she who needed comfort.

She was a child again, afraid of the dark. She conjured lurking things. Growling bears. Wintering snakes. A hungry pack of wolves nipping at her heels.

The hot flash rose from her belly into her chest and up through her forehead, burning her scalp. She'd seen it happen in the mirror in real time, a redness that flushed her cheeks and darkened the tips of her ears. She resisted the urge to throw off her coat, for she knew it was a false promise. The sweat coming next would make her cold—too cold. She would jump from fire into ice, and the woods would swallow her.

She stood, turned in a circle, sniffing the air for some hint of home. She breathed, and sweated, and waited until the flutter of wings above made her jump. It was impossibly loud, a cacophony of movement that vibrated the air. The kitten was roused from its nap, mewing and playing with the heartbeat that drummed inside Brea's chest.

She pointed the beam upward, searching half-naked limbs for the source of noise.

The hawk?

An owl?

A black silhouette absorbed the light. Elegant, dark wings flapped, settled, shifted from milky onyx to shades of blue-purple, then back to black. Wide, round eyes took Brea in, examined her. The crow's head tilted as if to challenge the woman. Its beak parted, but there was no caw-caw. Rather, a guttural rattle emerged, hot breath leaking into the cold air, a snake of smoke.

The rattle grew, shaking the world around Brea. She shifted the light, searching the canopy above. Dark bodies against jagged branches. So many, singing.

Rattling.

Shaking the trees.

Creating the mist with their breath.

Brea was frozen. The rattle hummed around her, calling down something sacred. Then all fell silent. And her flashlight went dark.

She drew in a shaky breath.

The waxing moon peered through the haze, its glow bringing the world to life. A thin blanket of ice crystals covered the trunks and fallen leaves; the woods were diamonds in the gleam. And Brea was able to make out the tree.

Our tree.

She knew where she was now—far toward the back of the property by the lake. It seemed impossible that she had walked that far—nearly five acres. And yet there it stood.

She had named it the giraffe, for that's what the silhouette appeared to be. Two separate trunks that merged into one. The legs sprouted from the ground, one tree bending to grow into the other—a pair of conjoined twins. The neck stretched up into the canopy as one entity, reaching for the sky. Brea imagined the roots under the earth intertwined, holding each other.

Just like us.

Brea had not thought of the tree since he'd passed. Emotion lumped in her throat and her heart's wound bled through her eyes. Her chest shook as she sobbed. The kitten purred. The crows rattled with her.

And she cried until she felt purged.

"I miss you," she said, her breath a rising trail. "I love you."

She stared at the space between the giraffe's legs. How many times had they imagined it was a portal to another world? A magic mirror. A curtain to Oz. She wished so much that it was. She would walk through it now if it would bring her to him.

"Not yet."

The woman's voice was a whisper on the wind. An oak leaf riding the currents, bringing with it the power of dreams. Brea's imagination opened, an eye in the center of her forehead. Deep knowing pulled the apparition to this side of the veil and the crows descended, opening the liminal space like a drape.

The elegant figure was wrapped in black—so dark it was almost blue in the moonlight. Her silver hair hung in jagged curls past her waist. It was tangled with browned leaves, twigs, and other things of the earth. She emerged through the giraffe's legs, birthed into the night, moving with careful grace, to stand before Brea.

The woman reached out a hand, brown and decorated with gnarled roots. Dark eyes glinted in the moonlight, deep pools that stretched through time. She was mesmerizing, enchanting.

Is this death, come to meet me in the woods?

Brea did not hesitate. She took her hand and was engulfed in a swirl of blue-black. The flutter of feathers was thunder in her ears, soft strands that tickled her skin, pulling her down, down into herself, where she flew in circles. Faster and faster she spun—a dust devil, a waterspout, a tornado.

Layers of time and memory unfolded—each a moment that had shaped her.

Childhood. Mama's voice. Bedtime stories. Kindergarten tears. Walks in the rain. Hot chocolate in a mug. Snow falling beneath streetlights. Jellybean trails and marshmallow peeps. Hot summer days sweet with melting popsicles. Daddy's guitar. Sibling laughter.

Playground bullies and best friends. Four square and jump rope. Softball and soccer grass stains. Singing in the spotlight. Grades and lunchboxes and square dancing in the gym.

High school hallways teeming with life. Choir and dance parties and sneaking out at night. Forbidden kisses. Wine coolers on her tongue. Deep friendship, intertwining souls. Secrets and late-night phone calls.

College dorm rooms. Homesickness. Shots in bars and borrowed cigarettes. Roommates and term papers and cramming. Bad relationships. Unexpected pregnancy.

Motherhood. Sacrifice. Lost scholarships. Nine to five. Bedtime stories. More kindergarten tears. Song and dance and laughter. Wet dog noses.

Heartbreak. Loss. Grief.

Hope. Prayer. Joy.

Degrees. New careers.

Finding herself again.

And finally, love. *Him.* Soulmates. Family. Nurturing. Birds in the trees. Dogs at our feet. New traditions. Bedtime stories. Cuddles on the couch. Wine and whiskey. Dreaming together. Holding hands by the fire. Grandchildren. Christmas wonder. Laughter. Their sanctuary.

And then...

Heartbreak. Loss. Grief.

The spinning stopped.

"And what now?" Brea asked. She wanted to scream but it came out in a choked whisper. "What now?"

She stood still, dizzy. Nausea rose. She sank to her knees, leaves crunching beneath her. She looked into the canopy above, branches still swirling out of focus. The moon, a moving target. And she began to sob, guttural sounds moaning out of her in wails, expelling the grief that had taken root in her belly. She gave it back to the Earth, for the Great Mother could handle such things. Sorrow leaked out of her and onto the forest floor.

The kitten mewed beneath her jacket as her sobs receded, and her breath shook.

"It's alright," Brea said, the words trembling in her mouth.

The apparition stood before her again, the feathered cloak draped around her like night. Long silver curls were an aura of woven stories. The secret-keeper. A shadow from the past and window into the future. Guardian of the veil between here and there.

"Your time is not yet done," she said.

Brea gulped. She knew this to be true, somewhere in the center of her body, of her soul. And yet, her mind fought it. Her heart wanted only *him*.

"You must let go," she said.

Brea shook her head.

No.

Long tears carved a trail down her face.

"I don't want to lose him," she said. His eyes, his face, his hands, his voice. All the tender things one hopes for in life. Now but a memory.

"You will never lose him," said the woman. Her voice was a whispering rattle. A low rumbling like thunder. "Love does not die. But you must release him from obligation. He may choose to walk with you in spirit, but not because you tether him. Free will. He has a journey, too, on the other side."

The words sank into Brea, unraveling the tight coil that strangled her heart. She had not considered this—that she might be impeding him. Grief gave way to a flood of love that engulfed her, rooting her to the Earth, springing from her fingers, warming her from the inside out.

The crow woman spread her dark wings, revealing a rainbow of plumage beneath. Red blood, orange sunset, yellow buttercup, green grass, blue sky, purple wildflower. She swayed, turning Brea in the opposite direction from before, unwinding her back through the labyrinth in a spiral dance. The colors distorted, melting together in a spectrum. Around and around she went, trees a blur, kitten mewing, crows rattling.

And in the distance, coyotes called.

Cried.

Howled.

It was the sound of wisdom. Of knowing. Of bending to spirit. Walking the line between life and death. Brea listened to the sanctuary they had found together. Trees spoke in chorus with the four-leggeds and winged ones.

And she chose love over fear.

Then all was still.

Brea stood at the fringe of two worlds, smelling the fires of home. The warm glow from the cabin beckoned her, and the beam from her flashlight was bright again. She was far from the giraffe, from the crow woman, from the foreign language of the trees. But the kitten was still nestled against her, purring.

Had the woods tricked her?

Coyotes called in the distance, their voices like cackling women in the night. "Yes," they said.

A smile turned up the corners of Brea's mouth for the first time in many days. As realization dawned, there was a rustle in the leaves. A large cat emerged, its eyes catching the flashlight's beam.

Mama.

The cat meowed. It was the sound of hope.

Brea reached inside her jacket and placed the kitten down, backing away gently. And in two breaths they were gone, just the echo of a mother's love as she carried her baby back into the night.

Brea stood for a moment, pondering the woods and their trickster ways. Wisdom was like that, luring one into new ways of knowing. It was never a straight line, but a twisted and convoluted path. A braided one. A labyrinth.

How she had needed this reminder to pull her from despair. Brea sighed. Her breath was still shaky from the tears, but her heart was full.

"Thank you," she whispered to the woods.

Our woods.

Brea turned toward home, with the flashlight illuminating the way. She stepped back through the thick blanket of dried leaves and ice crystals, out from the mist that clung to trunks and half-naked limbs. Past the crows, now dreaming. She hung between the worlds for just a moment, one foot in spirit and another rooted in life. And just as she was about to emerge from the mouth of the woods, she saw something curious in the flashlight's beam.

The long feather was dark blue-black. Shadow.

She knelt to pick it up, turning it over and over. Dark shifted into rainbow, and then back to night. What seemed to be one thing was more.

The luminescent spectrum was fractured light. The power of the sun captured from the sky, from the great beyond, singing songs only winged ones know.

Of birth.

Of death.

Of rebirth.

It vibrated in her gloved fingers, alive with magic. The wind woke, its cold chill licking her face. But she was warmer than she had been before tonight's journey.

Warmer than she had been in many moons.

With her flashlight in one hand and the crow woman's gift in the other, she headed back to the cozy hearth, a wet dog nose, and the knowledge that she still had work to do.

That she had been reborn.

And quietly, he walked beside her, guiding her home.

Just for a little while.

Until he could hold *her* again.

 This is a new short story created for this collection.

Ghost Apples

The crone called Eira emerged from warm darkness into winter air, breath dancing from her lined mouth in smoke. Cold tickled her nose and snow crunched beneath worn lambskin boots. The hush in the orchard stretched between trees and into the white sky, heavy with a promise of more weather to come. There was a telling ache in her bones.

Ice had fallen in daggers during sunset—first as a pelting rain, and then shards. As the cold seeped in more, it shifted to snow—large flakes diminishing into a fine mist. It turned the world into a looking glass; the snow was frosting, beginning to lift with short gusts of wind, swirling about in funnels, revealing the silver landscape beneath.

Her eyes skimmed the pristine view as she pulled the cloak tightly around her shoulders, its weight like powerful arms. The cowl tickled her neck, a reminder of the wolf brethren she had nurtured—so many litters now. Their fur was woven into the wool, adding to her magic. Some she had snipped from their tails as pups, others from the tips of their ears as they lay dying. They were each a piece of her now.

Bleddyn joined her at the threshold. His ears perked up, listening for sounds that did not belong. He sniffed the air, then looked to her as if to say, "danger." But she could already feel it—hunger reaching out with a forked tongue.

A predator. Cunning. Lurking. She would not wait for it to pounce.

They walked forward together, a bonded pair, the wolf on large paws with ready teeth, and Eira with a nocked arrow in her worn hands. Trees creaked with the weight of ice, their groans a base note to the tenor wind.

Bleddyn's nose led them to the edge of the orchard, where gusts lifted the blanket of snow from apple globes, ghostly echoes of the rotten fruit that remained after autumn. If the stories of Eira weren't enough, this site should frighten any man who trespassed. She'd only seen this enchantment once before—round icicles in the forms of apples that once hung. Even then, she had recognized the harbinger—something walking between the worlds. It had been on that night twenty-five years ago when a premature ice storm had borne down on them and the first Bleddyn had crossed into death.

Eira's breath caught in her throat at the memory, and the phantom apples whispered, drawing her closer. The clear surface was a curved mirror, showing things that had once been. Her reflection was distorted, pulling her back into the past. The folds above her eyes and the creases underneath seemed to disappear, revealing the fair face with which she had walked for many moons. Her gaze tore away from the apparition—her own ghost.

She would not be charmed. Not now. She was no fool.

Eira straightened and sniffed, then tightened her grip on the bow and arrow. She circled the tree, watching, waiting. There was a faint sound on the wind—the whimpering of an animal perhaps. Bleddyn sniffed and caught a new scent. As Eira followed him, passing beneath frozen shards and bowing limbs, she remembered.

The parts of herself that had long been discarded trailed behind in ribbons, encircling her with a quickened pace. She did not run, for she knew the ways of specters. You cannot outrun a memory. So, she relaxed and let them flood her, keeping her feet moving in the wake of Bleddyn's trail.

She was a girl—once. She was loved. There was a honeysuckle mama who lulled her to sleep with notes. And a papa bear with strong arms and a furry face. A baby brother with laughter like bubbles and tiny hands. And a warm home filled with apple pie, candlelight, and a warm hearth. But time leaves things behind, memories scattered like breadcrumbs, pecked away by sparrows.

Now she was a witch—an old hag. That was how the townsfolk had painted her, with no choice but to become it over time. Now she spent her days among the creatures, nestled in a wooden hut with no doors and no windows. There was no need to cover the thresholds for she was mother to all in the forest. They saw the vibrance within—something it had taken her a lifetime to find.

Eira had been a beauty—once upon a time. Boys watched, men lingered, women glared. The space of shelter inside her had become strangled by threads of friendship that turned into bitterness. Perhaps if she had been scarred or marked or disheveled in some way, they would have stayed beside her. But they whispered in low tones—never to her face. They did not know that words become spells when they have been spoken too many times.

But she did.

Eira was pulled from her dark reverie by Bleddyn's pause. He stood alert, sniffed at the air again, then ran.

Down the hillside they went, the wolf's gait at full speed with Eira trailing behind. She stumbled until she slid, trying to move with the curve of the land rather than resist it. When she came to a stop, she stood and shook the snow off. It was deep there, in the crevice surrounded by pines. Almost up to her knees. But Bleddyn was sure. There was something.

Where had he gone?

Eira scanned the landscape until she found his wolf form, sitting with patience beside a lump in the snow. She neared and saw it was a person—a girl—in a dark dress atop a red cloak.

No—not a cloak.

A red stain had spread on the white blanket beneath her. It leaked out from between her legs, a dark crimson in the center outlined by bright scarlet. Bleddyn nudged the girl's face and she stirred, a pale youth in a bed of dark curls. But when she opened her eyes, they grew wide. She sat up and backed away from the wolf, terror clear on her face.

Eira broke through shock which had frozen her upon discovering the bloody sight.

"He won't hurt you," she said, holding up her hands like she could freeze the moment. She crept closer, not wanting to alarm the girl. She removed her cloak and draped it over shaking shoulders, clothed only in torn underclothes.

The girl's downcast eyes released tears. Her lower lip quivered and a sob escaped. "The huntsman," she stuttered. "He— he..."

She could not say it. Her voice dissolved into whimpers.

"Attacked you?" Eira's eyes narrowed. She knew the blood was more than a moon cycle would be. The beast had violated her with trauma.

"Come," she said, helping the girl to her feet. "No one will bother you with my wolf leading the way. We must get you inside."

The girl did not protest.

Smoke rising from the hut guided them home, the smell of a warm hearth reaching out with ethereal fingers. Though it was not even mid-morning, the sky grew dark—another storm was on its way.

Eira supported the girl, walking beside her with a weak arm draped around her shoulders. Years in the forest had made her strong, but aging bones still complained under this new weight. The girl's eyes drifted ahead, looking for an answer that eluded them both. She was beyond even tears now. The huntsman had stolen more than her innocence. He had taken the very trust she had in the world and replaced it with bitterness.

Eira knew this well. She remembered, too.

It was in this state of violation she had been faced with a choice once—to crumble or to use fury as a weapon. This was how she had learned to yield her power. As a maiden, sensuality had become her poison—sweet, with a bit of tart, and a lingering scent of cinnamon. Manipulation was intoxicating revenge—for those who had always been enemies and even more seductive for those she had once called friends.

Soon the high was not enough. She sought more—searched for something sweeter, more succulent. Until she learned to add more herb and spice. Nettle, nutmeg, and clove. And the most potent ingredient—a drop of her own blood. It was magic that came with a price. One that turned her inside out until she could no longer recognize her own reflection.

Her fairness had become her undoing.

Outside of the hut, Eira pulled back the blanket that kept the warmth in—a simple drape with no lock or key—and guided the girl inside. They were enveloped in a smokey haze, sweet grass stoking the flames. Once she had given the girl a damp cloth and heavy blanket, she watched as the fair one drifted off into sleep, leaving the pain and misery behind in this world. She hoped sweet dreams would offer some comfort. For the crone would have none tonight.

The past jumped out from the shadows, in between the tongues of flame, in the wafting wind outside that howled like her soul. Phantoms from that night bared down on her, dancing round her head, tugging at her sash.

He had been a monster lurking behind a handsome face. Enchanting, luring, gentle—at first. But once he had hooked her with the swirl of a kiss, she was helpless in his grasp. She writhed, trying to slip out from under him, but with each protest he grasped tighter. She couldn't breathe. The rocking was like an unveiling of skin, layer by layer, unwrapping all she had woven in protection. Until it reached the inside—the softest part of her—the most hopeful. He drained it of joyful essence and replaced it with his desire. The maiden she had been was dead in an instant. She had no choice but to birth something else—something uglier.

Something wicked.

Eira's breath caught in her throat as she sank back into that moment, reaching through time to witness her own tragedy. It held her there, slipping further in, daring her to unleash the fury again. She breathed. The sweat beaded on her brow. And then she let it go.

Her mind sank back into wrinkled skin. Her hands reached up to her face, grateful that the once flawless flesh had aged. Each crease was a welcome change, for she now knew the truth. She could see with eyes wider than the sky. Beauty had been her bundle to carry—a lesson that wrote the story of her maidenhood. In the wake of violation and then so much obsession, so many desiring her—men, women, and everyone in between—she lost herself. It took her many years to realize that all they wanted was her creamy skin, raven hair, and eyes like the night. They knew nothing of the secret she was on the inside.

She turned once again to the girl, tucked into blankets and lost in slumber. For the first time, she was called to mother a human.

And her fury awoke.

"Bleddyn, stand guard," she said.

He circled the hut once, watching, knowing. He longed to follow. But it was not his time. Not yet.

He sat before the girl, ears perked, eyes steady. Eira saw her reflection in them, her form engulfed in the woolen cloak imbued with lupine essence. The love that passed between them was endless.

*

She bounded over the snow on light feet, concealed in the folds of the cloak. Flakes swirled in slowing wind, its voice only a whisper now. Clouds parted to reveal the full moon, caught between waxing and waning, spilling its light onto the white blanket below. It sparkled with magic, and Eira gathered it to her, weaving the light into her purpose.

She followed the scent of man, sharp and sour. Potent. She knew not how she had missed it before.

She passed through the orchard with its ghost apples, under ice-laden maples, and down the hillside to the pines where they had found the girl. Up the other side and into a grove of hemlock, where she came upon a cabin, smoke from its stack rising up to the moon as if to pull it down.

As if a man could.

Figures moved inside, backlit by the fire, casting shadows onto windows and beneath the doorframe. There was more than one.

Her upper lip quivered then bared teeth. The growl began in her stomach and stretched up through her throat. She tilted her head back in a howl that reached across the sky. It echoed through trees, into the hills and down into valleys. Then it returned to her—wolf brethren in chorus. Some voices she knew, others like distant memories from another life.

She was not alone.

Eira crept forward, the cloak encasing her, becoming one with her body. She descended, stealthy and focused. And she knocked.

Once. Twice. Thrice.

Then into the shadows she swept, no longer on two legs. And she waited for him.

The huntsman emerged from the cabin, stumbling. His silhouette swayed from side to side as he pulled suspenders back onto his shoulders, playing at stealth. He tried to rouse himself from the fog of a full meal and several drinks. But it was too late. Eira knew he was compromised.

"Who's there?" he said. An axe dangled from his hand, a weight that threw his balance.

The forest responded with silence. He took a few steps forward, down the stairs and into the snow. He glanced around the horizon, scanning it for a human form.

"Who is it?" The timid female voice emerged from within the cabin.

"Shhh!" His response cut the air as he turned, glaring in her direction. A moment passed and quiet sobs leaked through the open door.

Then the man returned his focus to the trees and paused, as if sensing a gaze upon him. Instinct cautioned him, pointing out his vulnerability, and he backed away toward the stairs. He faltered, stumbled.

It was all Eira needed.

With the moon at her back, she sprang. Four paws lifted her from the snowbank, her dark fur a shadow, her growl shaking the air, and she was upon him. Her teeth sank into his throat, releasing both warm liquid and garbled cries. She tore, she ripped, she drank.

Even when the pain pierced her back, she did not stop.

They fell upon the snow in a death dance, black and white and red blending into a swirl of struggle. And then he was still.

Eira rolled away from his grip, the taste of blood on her lips, the pain just starting to spread across her shoulders, down her legs. She tried to stand but faltered, then lay upon the snow-covered mother—the Earth that had held her in its womb when she had sought shelter from mankind.

Her eyes lifted to find a woman with long golden hair and a darkened eye. The knife was still in her hand. She was a wife trying to save her monster. The baby's cry from deep inside the cabin was the last thing Eira heard before she faded into the presence of those she had lost. She was one of them now—among her pack.

*

Bleddyn felt her slip away, across the veil to the other side, where those who had come before him dwelt. The sadness welled in his belly, emerged through his muzzle in a sorrowful howl. Others joined his song, over the hills, through the trees, their collective mourning intertwined.

The girl stirred, sat up, eyes wide. He had not meant to wake her.

He whined. Yawned. Approached her even as she backed away on the bed. But he lay beside her in his familiar spot and waited for acceptance.

When she placed a hand on his fur, the sorrow began to slip away, though he knew it would always remain as a murmur. The old woman's smell lingered and brought him comfort. It wasn't long before the girl's arm was tight around him, and her face was buried in his fur. Tears fell in drops, and with each one, he nestled into her crook. He was needed here, to guard. To help her remember. To survive.

And as he drifted further into dreams, he breathed more slowly, for he had a new mother now.

This piece originally appeared in *The Black Door*,
Pumpernickel House, 2024.

About the Author

Dr. Mary Carroll Leoson is a Lecturer at Middle Tennessee State University, Director of MTSU Write, and the author of YA novel *The Butterfly Circle* (Manta Press). She is also a Pushcart Nominee, Senior Editor at the *Journal of Creative Writing Studies*, member of the Horror Writers Association, and Co-Host of the Horror Writing Podcast, *Exhuming the Bones*. Her short fiction can be found in anthologies and literary magazines such as *Coffin Bell Journal*. When she's not teaching or writing about ghosts, you will likely find her in the garden or on the couch with her husband and two very spoiled dogs.

You can learn more at https://maryleoson.com.

Devil's Oak: Waking the Feminine Wound

Read and Follow

Digital PDF
https://doi.org/10.56638/mtopb00425

EPUB, Hardcover, and Paperback
https://www.lulu.com/spotlight/mtop

Goodreads
https://www.goodreads.com/book/show/239910520

MT Open Press Acknowledgements

Generous support has been provided by the following individuals and organizations:

Foreword + Review
Christopher Barzak

External Reviewers
Janet Alcorn
Jasmine De La Paz
Diane Sismour
Ada Wofford

Proofreading and Accessibility Testing Consultants
Katherine Aydelott
Ginelle Baskin
Joslin Boals
James Hamby
Lindsey Landrum
Lalonie McCarter
Victoria Frosheiser-Spurlin

Middle Tennessee State University
Operations and financial support from the James E. Walker Library:
Kathleen Schmand, Dean
Sean Strickland, Administration
Clay Trainum, External Relations

Consultations and operational support from:
Contract Office
Office of the University Counsel

Made in the U.S.A.

Short Story Collection Summary

Devil's Oak: Waking the Feminine Wound is a short story collection that features strong female characters against a backdrop of ghosts, fairy tales, and urban legends. The thirteen stories subvert the historical narrative of women in fairy tales, positioning them as bold and willing to step into the face of danger.

"The Braided Veil" features a young orphan in Victorian New Orleans who seeks revenge upon her mother's abuser.

"Devil's Oak" addresses the horrors of slavery through the eyes of a young girl who learns that her family owned human beings.

"Good Little Girls" takes readers back to childhood in which a sick girl explores her neighbor's attic on a stormy day; she discovers more than she bargained for.

"The Game" features relational aggression in the 1990's in a "mean girls" style that takes a grisly turn.

"Selkie Skin" leans into Celtic lore, following a young pregnant girl who longs for freedom.

"The Ripper Society" reaches back through time to Jack the Ripper's wife, who discovers his misdeeds and takes matters into her own hands.

"She Has Seen the Wolf" is a longer story that connects to my novel, *The Butterfly Circle*; when a graduate student learns she is pregnant, she uncovers her family's connected history to a haunted home for unwed mothers.

In "Roots in the Cove," a woman in an unhealthy relationship shapeshifts into a bear on a trip to Gatlinburg and finally finds her freedom.

Both "Marsh Girl" and "Cicadas in the Suburbs" explore the psychological challenges of suburban life, including postpartum depression and the longing for the magic of youth.

In "Honey Tree," a divorced woman seeks comfort from the bees, and in "Crow Woman," a widow faces metaphorical death and is reborn.

Finally, "Ghost Apples" is a retelling of Snow White from the perspective of the queen; she shapeshifts into a wolf to protect a young girl who has been attacked and seeks revenge upon her abuser.